THE FOOL REVERSED

THE FOOL REVERSED

Susan Whitcher

FARRAR STRAUS GIROUX

NEW YORK

Copyright © 2000 by Susan Whitcher
All rights reserved
Distributed in Canada by Douglas & McIntyre Ltd.
Printed in the United States of America
Designed by Filomena Tuosto
First edition, 2000
1   3   5   7   9   10   8   6   4   2

Library of Congress Cataloging-in-Publication Data
Whitcher, Susan.
  The fool reversed / Susan Whitcher. — 1st ed.
    p.   cm.
  Summary: Having started a relationship with a twenty-nine-year-old
poet while developing a friendship with a boy her age, fifteen-year-old
Anna is confused as she seeks to find and open the gateways of love
and poetry.
  ISBN 0-374-32446-8
  [1. Authorship—Fiction.   2. Interpersonal relations—Fiction.]
  I. Title.
  PZ7.W5774Fo   2000
  [Fic]—dc21   *99–16875*

For John,
and about time

Contents

THE FOOL REVERSED

SEX

Anna switched the tape recorder to *rewind*, then hit *play*. The zipping-backwards gabble choked and slowed to her own voice:

People think they're preparing you for what it's like, but they can't, really. Why don't they just leave a book on the table for you? But no, you've got to get The Talk. *It's some kind of parent's rite of passage, probably.*

My mother gave me the big sex talk about five years ago. We were just sitting in the car, in the parking lot of Jiffy One Hour, waiting—yeah, what an omen. Really.

My mother is so obsessive, she has to time her dry cleaning. And so, not to waste the jiffy hour, I guess, she pulls out her little spiral pad and starts drawing diagrams. See, here's the woman's insides, Anna. This is the uterus . . . here is her vagina. This is the man's . . .

Then she passes the pictures to me sideways, under the dashboard, like passing notes in school.

You really have to wonder what kind of gated community of the mind my mother thought we'd been living in. I was ten years old, for god's sake, I had two sisters in college! Or at least Vonda was by that time. Rennie was all over that baboon Keith in the laundry room after school, which if my mother didn't realize she must've been breathing too much dry-cleaning fumes. Everybody else in the building knew about it.

Well, we had The Talk, and I said Yuck or something vaguely appropriate at the juicy parts. What I was really thinking was, if Mrs. Park at the Jiffy handed me the box of lollipops, would my mother make me choose a sugarless one?

So then she says, "You won't feel that way when the time comes. When you're in the right relationship, Anna. Love will make you feel it's a beautiful experience."

I really, really hate it whenever somebody tells you that you're going to feel something like that, special. Like, you're going to love this, Anna. *Or,* you'll be so surprised. *Because then right away you know you won't be able to.*

Anna jabbed the *pause* button. She'd begun all wrong and wished she'd never made her vow not to erase. The vow was the first thing on this tape, along with some dumb-ass theory about the truth hidden in accident, something like that, meaning the things you said by mistake, not thinking, were the ones you really meant all along. By now she'd come to realize all that stuff was just drool. It came out of your mouth while your mind was utterly elsewhere.

I went to his apartment after school, Anna told the machine. Her fingers hovered above the buttons.

We were sitting on his futon drinking tea, and talking . . . I don't know how to tell this. I think I'm still in shock—

Pause. How incredibly mundane that sounded. She flopped back on her pillow and stared at the lightbulb in her ceiling. Now she saw blots of color everywhere. One of them turned out to be an actual ink stain on the knee of her pajamas.

On his futon, the long afternoon slotting through the blinds had streaked their bodies like tigers. They'd held delicate steaming cups of tea . . . For some inane reason she'd kept biting the rim of hers while he talked. It has no real taste, green tea. Only a fragrance.

He'd known before she did what was happening. He took the cup out of her hand. He touched her face, his fingers tracing the line of her cheek, then up under her hair so she had to bend toward him. And no, she'd felt no shock, not even plain surprise. It was more like being suspended in a vacuum, willing for whatever to happen . . . irresistibly.

The soft hiss of the tape machine recalled her thoughts. It ought to be so much easier to tape a diary than to write anything, a poem especially. Because a poem had to illuminate the whole universe in a flash of time, the way lightning sears its instant of vision into the retina. With a diary all you had to do was blurt out what happened and (hopefully) what you thought about it. She released the *pause* button, though she still hadn't decided what to say.

She said, *Today I made love for the first time.*

It had hurt. She might be still bleeding a little, though not as badly as, for example, when you skin your knee. At least with your knee you got to show off the gore, gain some glory, maybe.

Really, what she'd wanted to talk about on the tape was pain. There must be some connection that was necessary and cosmic between love and pain; otherwise, why have all those holy martyrs? It was like the way when you cut yourself blood wells up from your heart to fill the wound.

I used to think love was something you just fell into. Or somebody gave it to you, like the flu . . . flowers . . . what I mean is, now I understand love is something you have to make. *Like out of pain, and hope, and . . . For some reason, this is coming out utterly shallow and mundane.*

"Did I hurt you very much?" he'd asked, when they were lying side by side, not touching any more.

She'd opened her eyes and seen the gold was all rubbed off the afternoon. Their bodies that had been melting in sweat and radiance were dim now in the rumpled shadows of the bed.

He turned toward her, twisting the white sheet taut over his hip.

"You are as pale as an eggshell," he said.

She shook her head, no. Oh, no. The movement made her hair flop over one eye, and so must have spoiled the eggshell effect. She watched him through the dark strands for clues: a fine line etched between his brows . . . at the corner of his mouth a deeper, perhaps ironical, crease.

"You always seem so still and serene," he'd said.

So then she couldn't possibly say anything.

Anna gave up on the tape, for the time being at least. Sometimes it seemed that between the inside of her mind and the outside world there was this long, dim hallway. The hallway appeared empty and quiet, but the words starting down it got warped away somehow. They never made it safely to the lighted doorway at the end. When she was little, she'd had the same kind of feeling about getting up in the middle of the night to go down the hall to the bathroom.

She leaned over the edge of her bed and shoved the tape recorder underneath, where it would be hidden by the folds of the bedspread. The spread, with a pattern of clock-like roses in pink chenille, was a relic, like most of the other junk in her room, of her pre-conscious childhood. She really hated her room.

She got up and rummaged through her stash of writing materials for a sheet of silky onionskin bond paper, which she laid on the center of her desk. It would be better, after all, to write a poem.

She liked to keep the desk surface clear, like the mind freed for thought. All the stuff like papers or school binders had to go in the drawers, or underneath where it didn't show and fret at the edges of her concentration. She kept out the two copies of *Intus* and *The Keystone Review* that he had given her, with his pieces published in them. On top of these she laid a small glass paperweight with a blown bubble inside. If she lined it up just right, the bubble caught a gleam from the unshaded lightbulb in the ceiling and held it, like a star.

Incandescent

She wrote the word, then wondered if it wouldn't just make everybody think of lightbulbs. A lightbulb . . . As far as she remembered, the little wire inside glowed without burning up because there was a vacuum. If you cracked the glass around it, air would rush in, and the filament would instantly flare up and die.

After maybe half an hour of staring at the single word on the blazing-white page she realized she had nothing more to say. She went down the hall to the bathroom, where she stared at the small pink stain on her underpants. Then she wandered into the kitchen to find something edible, but there wasn't anything, so she went to bed.

FATE

In her dream she was riding a bicycle downhill, wind rushing in her nose. The road bumped, she jerked back the handlebars. Now she was swooping up, up—actually flying! The ground spun away below.

Anna woke. It was morning and she remembered she didn't know how to ride a bike.

Her father had tried to teach her once. They went to the park with Vonda's old blue Royal that had silver streamers on the handlebars. Anna had been too little to reach the handlebars and the pedals both at the same time. She'd clung to the hard rubber handgrips while her father pushed.

Don't let go, she called, trying to keep her feet up so the pedals coming round wouldn't strike her.

Don't worry, he said.

But Anna's father always did let go of people sooner or later. She'd had one glorious plunge downhill, off the path and through woods, while the wind crackled the silver streamers.

That was how she'd got her scar. Lying in bed, Anna touched it with the tip of her tongue, a tiny stiff check mark above her lip.

So now, she thought, *I'm having an affair with a man fourteen years older than me. Almost twice my age.* Probably some disaster would happen, but there was nothing she could do. She just kept hurtling along, waiting for fate to smack her in the mouth.

The phone was ringing in the kitchen. Her own phone she'd unplugged and stuffed under the bed with all the other extraneous trash that used to clog her space.

It's him, she thought, not moving, hope driving through her like nails.

He'd only ever called her once before. That time she wasn't home. Her mother had answered the phone. Afterwards, there'd been questions . . . What would she say this time? *He's my sex partner. We had sex.*

Anna kicked back her covers, yelling, "Don't get that, it's for me!"

No answer.

She skated down the hall to the kitchen—"I've got it!"—grabbed the doorframe, grabbed the phone off the hook—"Hello?" The phone receiver tangled in its cord. "Hello!"

"Oh, hi. It's me, Pauline. You sound all out of breath."

"I—was asleep."

"Well, it's almost lunchtime." Pauline had called to say they could get a ride tonight with her cousin. "I told him, drop us off at Caffè Mezzaluna. He's cool . . . He won't tell."

The Caffè Mezzaluna was really a wine bar. On Saturday nights its special feature was an open-mike stage. Interestingly maladjusted types read poetry, or sang, or otherwise made asses of themselves.

"Come on," said Pauline, slyly. "We might see Thorn there."

"He won't read at those things."

"He did, once."

Which was true, that was how they'd first met him, the only real poet among the posers.

The single poem Thorn had read that night told the story of a Chinese monk, Li Hyejung, confined in isolation for spreading anti-government lies. His cell was a tiny, windowless box that had once been a community bread oven.

On the first day of his imprisonment Li Hyejung counted all the clay tiles that lined the old oven walls. There were eighty-four. After that, he permitted himself to touch only one tile each day, meditating on it, exploring it with his fingers in the dark, tasting it with his tongue. Some days he would stroke and sing to his tile like a baby, or a lover. Some days he pounded it with bloodied fists.

On the eighty-fourth day, Li Hyejung died, exultant, having mastered all truth.

When Thorn stopped reading, it seemed to Anna that the whole café full of people and chairs and clanking plates and jostling conversations had gone mute. Even now in her imagination Thorn appeared as if on a darkened stage, his profile hard-edged by a spotlight. His eyes were gray, his nose proud like the beak of a Viking ship, his dark blond hair pulled smooth with a rubber band.

In fact, the Caffè Mezzaluna had no real stage, only a raised place in one corner with a standard lamp.

Pauline was asking could Anna get out tonight.

Anna said, "I guess . . . I don't think my mother's even home to ask."

"Then what's the problem? You sound all weird," said Pauline. "Did something bad happen with you and Thorn?"

All Anna's memory strings twanged so she shivered *yes*. "Yes, something's happened. But not bad."

"Oo. Spill all," commanded Pauline. But then she changed her mind and told Anna, *Wait*. "Bring the cards over to my house. I want to do a reading, ream out your tight little soul."

"You make that sound incredibly obscene."

Pauline laughed her evil vampire laugh and hung up.

Anna sighed and scratched her stomach under the waistband of her pajamas, then picked up the tented note her mother had left on the kitchen counter, beside the phone. What a surprise, she'd gone in to work on a Saturday again. *Don't wait up . . . Two lamb chops in the freezer.*

So Thorn could've called if he wanted, Anna thought, unfairly. How could he know her mother wasn't home on a weekend? She swallowed the little bubble of disappointment that came up, like something from her stomach.

She went back to her room and got out the deck of tarot cards. She kept the cards wrapped in a green silk scarf, the sea-green of jade.

After smoothing the bedcovers, Anna sat down cross-legged and spread out the square of silk. The cards tumbled out, right side up, upside down, all the mystical images: cups, wands, swords, pentacles, sun, moon, priestess, king, death. Some stood for possible events, some for stages in the journey of your life. The latter were mainly the named cards, like the tower or the star. They were the major arcana. Court cards, like a king or knight, stood for real people. Eyes closed, Anna stirred the cards with her right hand, then picked one. She psychically conjured it to be the knight of cups.

She opened her eyes and saw she was holding the fool. She tossed it back on the heap and stirred again, this time with her left hand. Thorn looked like a medieval knight. Anna visualized his long pale hands lofting a jeweled cup. She shut her eyes and chose . . .

The fool again. This was too weird. She studied the image on the card: a carefree youth setting out on a journey. He wore an embroidered tunic with long fluttery sleeves, a feather in his cap. The fool was gazing at the sky, but you could see he was about to step off the edge of a cliff.

Also, she was holding the card upside down, which changed the meaning. Anna slotted it between her toes. She flopped back on the bed and waved the fool in the air.

It was a card about making choices, about getting started with life, the first of the major arcana. The fool stood for a person's spirit in the moment before it stepped down into the real world, the world of bodies and events.

But upside down? Maybe she'd step off the cliff and land on her head. Or else she'd make her life's journey in reverse, unraveling like a ball of string.

The card fluttered from Anna's toes onto the floor.

So, what had she been expecting anyway, a dozen red roses, shrink-wrapped in plastic and delivered to her door? With maybe a singing telegram, *Dreaming of you the morning after . . .*

Thorn utterly despised generic sentiment. And he had to be careful, now more than ever since they'd had sex. Maybe she would see him tonight, at Caffè Mezzaluna.

Maybe he'd be there with other friends. Anna didn't mean to whine, because basically she accepted that Thorn lived in a different world, one that she could enter (like the enchanted castle in a fairy tale) only by stealth. In that enchanted world he had work, grownup friends, even an ex-fiancée.

Anna slithered her foot across the pile of cards. Elaine, the queen of swords. She was an older woman, a business person who ran some kind of import gallery downtown. Originally, when Thorn came out west from New York for his sabbatical year, he'd planned on living with her. They'd separated since, obviously, but Elaine's name was still on the buzzer to his apartment. They still saw each other sometimes.

Anna thought probably she should get up now and at least wash her hair. She slipped her hands down under the band of her pajamas and thought how weird it was that these were *her* hands touching her stomach, her thighs. She felt like Thorn was still inside her. Not . . . *that way.* Like some clot of undissolved excitement.

She still had hours and hours to wait until tonight, when she could really step into the world of bodies and events. Maybe she wouldn't get up yet. Pauline could wait for her awhile. If she lay still and remembered minute by minute all of yesterday, what he had done and said—how she had felt—it might start to seem more real to her. Now it was like some scene illuminated by too bright light. There were no shadows, no buildup of familiar feelings, to give substance and meaning to the outlines.

Or maybe she'd just try playing solitaire with the tarot cards.

Pauline had given Anna the tarot deck, way back in the summer before she ever met Thorn. How Pauline got it was, she stole it at the Saturday market.

One Saturday last summer Anna had been standing at the bus stop down by Westview Thriftway, vaguely planning on riding downtown. A red car pulled up in front of the stop and Pauline slid out from the passenger side.

"Oh, good," said Pauline when she saw Anna. "Act like you were expecting me, O.K.?"

"O.K.?" Pauline yelled at her mother in the red car. She made shooing motions until the car pulled slowly away into traffic.

Anna waved at it.

Pauline said, "I told her I was meeting a friend here, so she wouldn't think I was taking the bus alone. My mother is so unplugged, you know she thinks I'll get STDs just from sitting on public-transportation seats . . ."

That was how Anna began to be friends with Pauline. Of course she'd known her before from school, but they weren't friends. Anna saw Pauline had cut her pale blond hair short and shaved up the back since school had ended. The effect, together with tiny golden freckles and black eye shadow, was like undead Christopher Robin.

The bus came, and they got on. Pauline slid down her spine on the plastic seat and stuck her long legs across the aisle. She let her coat flop open. Even though it was summer, Pauline was wearing a thrift-store fur jacket, bald at the cuffs, with a big hand-lettered joke button on the lapel: THE FIRST PERSON TO WEAR THIS COAT IS ALSO DEAD. Pauline was vegan.

The only other people on the bus were some junior gangbanger types, probably from River City. They climbed over seats, hooting and trying to get Pauline's attention, but she just stared off into the void.

Making a feeble attempt at wit, Anna asked didn't the criminal type appeal to her?

"Oh, please. The one thing I despise . . ." Pauline let her head fall back against the seat. "I totally despise stereotypical conformity."

"Maybe you could go for a lonely suicide bomber."

"Suicide is sexy."

Anna was noticing how Pauline's irises were almost without color, like pond water. Like soap bubbles. They held reflections.

Pauline said, "Where're you going, anyway?"

"I thought maybe City of Books . . ."

"No, let's don't go there. Let's go to the Saturday market and eat elephant ears. God, I'm so addicted to those things, aren't you? Anything made out of fried dough."

Anna said actually she thought they were nasty.

"That's the point, duh. It's a death wish. I've got to get in there and glob up my arteries before too much blood makes it to my brain. Otherwise, there's just too much grief in life, you know?"

The bus let them off in the cavernous place beneath the Bournwell Bridge. Pauline huddled her coat close against the dank air greasy with diesel fumes and the smell of onions frying.

"Let's get out in the sun," she said.

They walked along old trolley tracks, avoiding the sidewalk, where homeless men shared bent cigarettes. Out in the square, summer light and heat returned full force. Radios blared. Gulls off the river screamed over a carton of spilled french fries.

Pauline said, could you believe all these gut buckets scarfing dead animal parts. She meant the tourists buying hot sausages and teriyaki sticks from the vendors' trucks.

Anna asked if she still wanted elephant's ears, since it seemed like Pauline could get her grease fix just by breathing the saturated air.

"I don't have any money, anyway," said Pauline. "Do you? Let's go look at the bazaar."

They entered under an archway of tie-dyed T-shirts into a maze of stalls pitched end-to-end or cobbled together with wa-

vering walls and tunnels made of Indian bedspreads. Everything reeked of incense. Unless you frantically desired some
hemp jewelry or patchouli massage oil, the main reason for
coming here was to make the scene. People dressed for it,
bared their tattoos for it, brought along their guitars and their
bongs.

Pauline started riffling through a rack of vintage clothes. She
half pulled out a sateen cowboy shirt and draped her fur coat
over the hanger. Underneath she was wearing a little kid's
T-shirt that barely stretched past her rib cage. It had a picture
of a World War II bomber on the front.

"I was fucking melting to death in there," she said.

Anna warned her that somebody would take her coat.

"No they won't. I wish I had decent tits. You are so lucky,
Anna."

In response, Anna's voice malfunctioned, which annoyed her
a lot, because obviously Pauline only said what she did to catch
her off balance. Anna was sensitive about her bust.

"I think the last time any guy looked me in the eye was in
fourth grade," she told the rack of limp vintage sleeves.

"Well, how can they? You walk around with your head down.
Stick your shoulders back, show what you've got."

"What I've got is a self-esteem issue, O.K.?"

"O.K.," said Pauline. "You like essential oils?" Now she was
running her hands over a row of tiny bottles on a stall flashing
with crystal prisms. "What kind do you like? How about
heliotrope? Or frankincense?"

"I never know what you're supposed to do with those."

Pauline shrugged. "Pour it in the bath. Light a match to it.
Stick it up your nose."

Anna was watching a fat old man playing on a cardboard guitar. He hummed and staggered from side to side, so his white satin cape swished and the guitar neck nodded time. At first she thought he must be drunk, but then she realized he was just Elvis. He wore white jewel-studded boots. He made her feel sad.

Pauline decided she wanted a beer. "Come on, there's a tent over near the fountain."

Anna said, "Nobody's going to sell you a beer."

"No, but somebody'll buy me one. You watch."

"I don't even want to see this."

"I don't even want to see this," Pauline mimicked, pulling in her chin and squinting down her tiny spangled nose.

Anna said with as much dignity as a person can who's suddenly been confronted with the transmuted ghost of her mother that she'd meet Pauline by the fountain later.

"Yeah, O.K." Pauline's weird clear eyes were already focusing on something way off beyond Anna. "Don't get stolen," she added.

Walking away, Anna experienced a strange sensation. If you've ever tried pushing the backs of your hands as hard as you can against a doorframe, after a few minutes if you step away from the door your hands will float up all by themselves, like wings. It seemed to Anna that she and Pauline had been shoving against each other for the last two hours. Now her ego rose and expanded cloudlike. She floated toward the fountain. You could get addicted to a feeling like this, Anna thought.

This part of the square was faced by tall nineteenth-century storefronts with elaborate white plaster work, like a row of wedding cakes. You could still buy river charts here, and coils of rope and hardtack in ten-pound tins. The fountain was a white marble basin filled by three identical bronze Greek maidens pouring out water pots.

Anna stepped up on the rim of the basin and tried out a Greek maiden pose. She was not really the statuesque type. She was small, her hair was lank and dark, and her legs were skinny.

She caught the eye of some guy in a fortune-teller's stall.

"Come pick a card," he called to her.

Anna jumped down off the fountain. She shook her head, raising her hands in a thanks-but-no-thanks gesture. But he called, *Hey, no charge.* So she decided, *why not?*

His stand displayed four or five different styles of tarot cards, ranging from goddess/feminist to fantasy pornographic, plus dangling pendants, candles, incense. Anna saw one really interesting thing, the real skull of some animal with twisting horns. It looked prehistoric.

The guy himself looked more like he ought to be passing out Bible tracts than dabbling in the occult. He wore his hair gelled straight back, so you could see the comb tracks in it. He was a hand kneader, a deep eye gazer.

He said his name was Wayne. He kneaded her hand. Then with a showman's gesture he swept up the cards laid out on his counter and fanned them out again, face down, for Anna to pick. He told her to lay her hands on the cards first, shuffle them around as much as she wanted, concentrate on her life situation.

Anna stared at the silver pentacle on a thong around Wayne's neck. It flashed when his Adam's apple bobbled. She wasn't even sure if she had a life situation. She had no problems, particularly, unless you counted boredom. No relationships. What she had seemed more like a chrysalis than a life.

He said, "When you're ready, choose a card. Hold it in your right hand."

The card she chose was the lovers. It showed an angel spreading its wings above a woman and a man. They were naked and displayed huge, painstakingly detailed sexual parts. Wayne was using one of the juicier tarot decks.

"Ah, the lovers," he said. "A new relationship is beginning for you."

"Not a chance!"

Anna spoke, laughing, those actual words. Maybe her psychic vision had been blunted by embarrassment. Anyway, since that day she'd come to understand intimations of fate were like pictures taken by the Mars probe, or sonograms of unborn babies. *See*, people would tell you, *there is evidence of ancient life.* Or, *there's his little head.* You looked and looked, and you believed, but you didn't see anything.

Wayne told Anna she might meet somebody soon. "I usually see like a two-, three-month time frame for my readings. Or this could be more of an internal thing. See here, the man—the man gazes at the woman. He's like your conscious mind, gazing into your heart. Your deeper thoughts." He screwed up his eyes as if he, too, gazed at something deep inside Anna. "But the woman, see, she's looking up at the angel. The angel stands for Higher Guidance. It's a warning to choose wisely—"

"Or else go on the pill," said Pauline, appearing suddenly beside Anna. She was holding two full and sloppy plastic cups of beer. "Want one?"

"Oh . . . no thanks."

"You can have it, then," Pauline told Wayne.

He smiled at her like she'd given him something truly marvelous, a gift of wisdom or of love.

Anna asked how she could know if the card meant a real person she was going to meet, or just her consciousness and stuff.

"I mean, even if it is inside myself, how would I know what's the particular thing I'm supposed to choose carefully about?"

Wayne said he could do a full reading if she wanted. But that wouldn't be for free, of course. He charged fifteen dollars.

Even though Anna had asked the question, he was answering Pauline. Pauline had that effect on people. Like a hologram— No matter how much you understood intellectually that other people were standing right beside her, Pauline always seemed somehow closer to the eye. The other people became background.

They hung around Wayne's stall a while longer. Pauline had to pick a card, and then a couple more because the first one was too boring. Wayne told Pauline about finding the curly-horned skull in the mountains and meditating on it, so it became his shaman animal. Anna bought a paperback on reading fortunes with the tarot cards. She would've liked to get some cards, a classic Rider deck, but they cost too much money.

Later, as they wandered back across the market, Pauline told Anna she ought to learn how to do that tarot shit. "You'd be good at it. You've got the look, way out of it—" She flickered her fingers like wings flying away. "Much better than Mr. Breathe-in-your-face back there."

Anna said, *why not*. For a summer job it beat Papa's Pizza, which is what Rennie and Vonda used to do. Secretly she felt hugely flattered that Pauline would think about her in that way. She flirted with a vision of herself, hollow-eyed, garbed in trailing velvet, her white hands floating above the mystic cards.

But then she said, "Probably I'll be too busy eloping with my man of destiny."

"Huh? Oh, you mean the naked guy."

"Maybe I'll go with the angel."

They collected Pauline's coat, since nobody had bought it yet.

"Thank god," said Pauline. "Like, I am dying for some pockets here." She sucked in her stomach so she could rummage inside her pants. First she brought up a paisley bandana, then a little bottle of essential oil, frankincense. "I mean, if it was good enough for Jesus, right?" She was still fishing around. "Uh-oh, I think the elephant ears got too squished . . ." Pauline burst out laughing. "You believed me! Here, these are for you. Go on, take them. They're tarot cards, stupid."

Anna felt ambushed. All that time she'd been standing around, basically despising the fortune-teller, she had actually been participating in a crime against him. He should have been despising her.

She said, not to be a prude but she really didn't want the cards. She said, *take them back to what's-his-face*, though they both knew that was impossible. Later she said Pauline should keep them and the book, too.

Pauline said, "Oh, God, now you think I'm like a total klepto, don't you? The thing is, I really, truly want to be a nice person, you know? Like I wanted to give you a present. This is so hard."

Anna muttered, *That's O.K.*

"Yeah, I know. Anyway, I can't keep them, on account of my mother."

Pauline's mother was one of those people who think fortune-telling, and practically everything else including the Pope, is devil worship. Anna wouldn't have guessed that about her, seeing the red car.

After the market Anna and Pauline went back to Pauline's

town house, which had all white furniture and carpeting in the kitchen. Pauline fixed them iced cappuccinos with an iced-cappuccino machine, and they ate stale cheese popcorn. These foods were O.K. for vegans, Pauline explained, because of being totally made of chemicals.

Pauline showed Anna a framed studio portrait of her mother on the bookshelf in the living room. Pauline's mother wore a tiny gold cross that dangled in her cleavage.

"She got breast enhancement after the divorce," Pauline said. "Plus, she got born again. That's why you have to keep the cards."

Anna said her father was a Catholic, with the Pope and everything. She could remember being little, toddling behind her sisters on the way to St. Pius Church, "all three of us in big white fluffy dresses, like a line of ducks."

Religion hadn't stopped her father from divorcing, either. Or from sleeping with every woman he could get his hands on since.

Anna bit down on a piece of popcorn. It deflated slowly, like a punctured tire.

"Sticks to your teeth," said Pauline, picking at hers. "I'm addicted to it when it gets like this. You're lucky your custodial's not religious."

"My mother? No, she's more your basic soulless bureaucrat type."

Anna stirred through the tarot cards spread out on Pauline's coffee table. It was the Rider deck, with pictures like the illustrations in old books of fairy tales. She really did want them. Still, somewhere on the bottom layer of her conscious thought, under all the pages of unfinished poems and discarded beliefs, lay a suspicion that some day God was going to make her pay.

POETRY

Naturally, it was Pauline who had first discovered the Caffè Mezzaluna, listed under "nightclubs" in the Weekend Life section of the paper.

"It says they do poetry readings," she told Anna. "We should go."

To which Anna had replied, "And you are on . . . what?"

But actually Anna herself had been the cause of Pauline's sudden interest in poetry or, more exactly, poets. Anna had insisted on reading aloud to her one utterly inspiring paragraph out of *The White Goddess* by Robert Graves. Graves wrote that the true function of poetry is to summon the muse. But the poet's muse is also the Goddess, and you know for sure when She arrives, because you're seized with an ecstasy, a rising up of the hairs of your head, an exultant terror.

Anna knew for a fact that even some of her own stuff, when she read it over to herself aloud, produced a little shiveriness.

It was the idea of men grappling with ecstasy that had appealed to Pauline. And with Pauline, the leap from idea to action happened like electricity arcing. It could leave you feeling

just as buzzed and stunned as any other spark, divine or otherwise.

Anna, grasping as usual at the mundane, said, since it was a
nightclub they couldn't get in, anyway. "It doesn't say 'all ages,'
does it?"

But secretly she felt wildly intrigued. She'd never been to a
nightclub, or a poetry reading. She let herself get sucked into
arguments over strategy: how to infiltrate, what to wear, what to
tell their assorted mothers.

They told Anna's mother to drop them off at the Arthouse
Cinema on Bellona Avenue. As they walked the six remaining
blocks to Caffè Mezzaluna, they were still arguing.

"I know exactly what kind of jerk-off artist we're going to
find at this place," Anna said. "It's going to be, like, karaoke
poetry."

Anna was suffering high-expectation backlash. She'd made
the mistake of showing one of her own poems to Pauline.
Whenever she showed somebody a poem, if they loved it a lot
she felt annoyed with them for being stupid or insincere. But
if they didn't love it enough (like Pauline), she felt crushed.
Maybe what she really feared was that the poets at Caffè Mezzaluna would turn out a bunch of asinine posers, and they'd all
be better than her, anyway.

Pauline said, "Now take off your shirt."

"What?"

"You're wearing that sexy tank under your shirt. It'll make
you look older."

"Well, what am I supposed to do with this?" said Anna, re-
luctantly unbuttoning her flannel.

"Tie it around your waist. Hurry up, that's the place."

Pauline took Anna by the elbow and steered her across the street, toward where they saw tables set out on the sidewalk. A knot of people hung around the café entrance. Some brandished drinks; others were just arriving, trying to push inside. The door swung continuously, scattering snatches of laughter and music.

Anna didn't notice anybody stamping hands. But a waiter hovered near the door. Maybe he was just minding the outside tables. She tried not to catch his eye. She felt Pauline's fingers tighten on her arm.

Suddenly Pauline shrieked, "Oh my *god*, I left my *purse* under the table!"

Pauline hauled Anna through the door. The waiter called out after them. Anna kept her head down and muttered excuses as Pauline rammed her through a wall of bodies.

Pauline went on screeching, "Oh my god, there it *is*! Somebody's *sitting* at our *table*—"

"We're going to get arrested," Anna said.

Pauline did the "Scream" face, clutching the sides of her head, dragging her mouth down.

Pauline had shaved off the rest of her hair for this occasion, so for an instant the image was perfect. Looking at her, Anna wondered if maybe she was anorexic. Pauline talked constantly of food, but her cravings seemed mostly for things that were basically inedible.

"I am fucking dying for an iced cappuccino," Pauline said.

For some reason, this struck Anna as hilarious. Soon they were both laughing so hard some guy at a nearby table tipped back his chair to listen in. His friends hooked two chairs over from another table so Pauline and Anna could sit down. The guy ordered a bottle of Greek wine and extra glasses.

"See, what did I tell you," Pauline said to Anna. "Easy."

"Absolutely," the guy agreed randomly, flashing white teeth in a black beard.

Anna sat next to a woman named Moira. Moira's clothes were covered with beads and fringe. As she talked, she constantly gathered up and redistributed tag ends of fringe, slithering scarves, wisps of frizzy pale hair. She reminded Anna of a heap of loose sand.

Besides Moira there were three men, all old, possibly even in their thirties. They'd all bought their clothes out of the kind of catalogue that features men their age posing as wild and carefree college students. The one who'd ordered the wine had tight dark curls showing at the neck of his shirt. When he laughed, he pointed his beard at the ceiling and barked sharply.

These people seemed pretty typical of the crowd. Twisting around, Anna spotted a sprinkling of goths and the odd draculoid, plus one or two actual suits. On the low platform that served for a stage, a wand-like youth sang plaintive ballads. As he stood up to take his bow, his guitar whacked against the reading lamp. Anna suffered a sudden random vision of Elvis with his cardboard guitar at the Saturday market.

Next on stage came a man wearing a studded leather jacket. In spite of the flashy jacket, he had the vaguely squashed look shared by leftover cupcakes and guys that nobody wants. He read a long poem about how he'd raped the Virgin Mary— though possibly he was talking about corporations wasting the rain forest.

The wine-buying man turned out to be some kind of editor or magazine publisher down from Seattle. The other people at the table were suck-ups who wrote. Pauline told everybody Anna wrote poems, too, so they all stared at her for a moment with eyes politely glazed. The editor tried to refill her glass, but it was still full.

Anna smiled reflexively. She licked the rim of her glass. The wine smelled something like Christmas trees, only sour. She watched Pauline flirt.

Judging from her performances at school, Pauline's approach to guys was pretty much like the way she ate. She'd seize ravenously on some low-nutrient variety. Anna didn't know Pauline well enough yet to say if she actually slept with the guys or just twisted them into crumbs, then brushed them off.

Recorded music played during a break in the readings. Pauline got up to dance with one of the guys from the table. Anna stood up, too, saying, *Excuse me a minute.* She planned to find a restroom, then maybe take a long while getting back. She discovered a corner where there were armchairs (all occupied) and racks with newspapers and small-press magazines for sale. She wondered if one of them was the barking editor's. She noticed a woman asleep in one of the armchairs who looked like an ordinary bag lady off the street. Maybe she had poems stuffed into one of her bags.

Anna flipped through a magazine. Behind her on the stage some woman declaimed in a twangy Kentucky accent about hard times for the women on the farm. They seemed to wade around in pools of darkly feminine blood. Anna turned and was surprised to see she was Moira.

Eventually Anna went back to the table. There was somebody new sitting in her place. The others were all telling him he should put his name on the sign-up sheet to read some poems. But he only shook his head, smiling down into his wineglass, twisting the stem between his fingers.

Anna noticed his hands right away, how long the fingers were, and pale, but at the same time strong-looking. Like they could be a sword fighter's hands.

The editor said his name: Thorn Arneson. He was an actually published poet, and he taught college someplace back East. Thorn looked up at Anna, his eyes gray like stainless steel, like a knife blade catching the light. He said something—Anna didn't even remember what he said. *Oh, I'm sorry, did I take your place.*

Anna stood speechless, afraid that if she moved or spoke he might take flight, like a great rare hawk startled from its branch. Helplessly, she felt her body distorting under his gaze. Her skull expanded hot and light, her breasts bloated like dough.

Afterwards Anna often wondered, did it happen then, at first sight? Or later, while she listened to him reading the Chinese poem? Why didn't she recognize that it was love that was happening to her? She only knew she'd been wounded somehow—stabbed; she felt the point of the knife drag against every breath she drew.

Somebody pulled out Moira's chair for Anna. Thorn did not speak to her again, or seem to notice her at all except for one flickering glance when the editor referred to Anna as "a poet." She would never, ever have called herself that, to him of all people. In her lap, her hands felt like cold raw chickens.

Thorn called the editor Dex. Thorn was saying, "Dex, give it a rest. I won't do stand-up in a bar, it's whoredom."

Dex answered, "This little lady wants to hear you read, man. How about that Chinese dissident piece you showed me at dinner?"

Thorn frowned. "He was a monk. Li Hyejung."

"Just listen to your editor: never disappoint a woman."

Anna assumed Dex meant Pauline, but then he plopped his hand on her own bare shoulder.

Anna bolted up, babbling excuses. They were going to think she had some bladder disease, always on the run. The hand slid off her arm, like hot fresh spit sliding down a wall.

All the time Thorn was reading his poem, Anna lurked behind the rack of magazines in the armchair corner. She wondered, was it too abysmally self-absorbed to imagine he might be reading for her? Because Dex had said she'd be disappointed. So why hide, why couldn't she sit up and smile like a normal person? Pauline would be pissed as hell at her. Pauline already thought she was feeble in social situations.

Anna kept away from the table until it was past time for them to leave. Her mother would be parked in front of the movie theater, eyeballs pasted to her watch.

When she finally did go back to collect Pauline, she found Thorn there again. He had a way of veiling his eyes, which would suddenly lift and flare if something caught his interest. Anna sat down abruptly in an empty place beside Pauline.

Anna wanted to look at Thorn, to examine him closely. How old was he? Twenty-five? More? Twenty-seven? Was he still looking at her? Anna studied the black hairs on Dex's hand.

Dex sat with his arm draped over the back of Pauline's chair. His fingers brushed the delicate pale knobs of her spine. He chatted with Thorn about an exhibition of Chinese art that was opening at some gallery downtown.

Thorn said, "Anna. You should come. I can put your name down on the guest list for the opening."

His voice was very beautiful, light and gentle, but with a teasing edge that shredded her concentration. She could think of nothing to say except, inanely, "Why?"

"Because I think you'll enjoy the pieces."

Anna bit off another *why*. She managed a slight cryptic smile.

"I'll write the date and address down for you, shall I?"

Pauline said, "You can write it on my hand."

Stupid Anna! Why hadn't she understood he meant them both, Pauline too? Her eyes flew up and met his, alight with laughter—at herself? At Pauline? He might think they were competing for attention, like grade-schoolers with a favorite teacher. But somehow she already knew he wore laughter and mockery lightly, like a garment he could slip off. Underneath, his expression would still be serious.

He reached across the table to take Anna's hand and wrote on the palm with a gold-tipped pen. She curled her fingers over the writing.

Later, walking back up Bellona Avenue, Pauline asked did Anna want to go to that Chinese art place.

Anna lied and said, "Not really."

"Is your mom going to be pissed we're not at the movie?"

"Probably. But I told her half an hour late on purpose, so the theater'll be closed. We can say we got tired of waiting and took a walk."

Anna's mother rarely proved difficult to manage. After surviving Rennie's and Vonda's adolescence, she hadn't much energy left for Anna's.

For the rest of the way till they spotted the car, Anna and Pauline made fun of David Dexter Fromm, the editor, alias "sexy Dex."

Anna lied again the next day when she told Pauline she'd by mistake washed the gallery's address off her hand.

The Song Gallery's exhibition of Neo-Traditionalist Chinese ceramics opened on Labor Day weekend. There had been a notice about it in the paper. Anna went late, so as not to seem too eager. Then she almost didn't make it at all because she'd failed to allow for the slow holiday bus schedule. As she hurried into the air-conditioned gallery, her shirt turned clammy with cold sweat.

She saw Thorn right away. He stood at the back of the room, chatting with a group of Chinese people. Anna immediately began to study glass cases with intent, opaque eyes.

For two weeks she'd been living on the points of knives, not knowing for sure if she had somehow made him up. Now there he stood. He was laughing, his head back, the laughter running down his throat into the open collar of his shirt. His eyes were rather close-set, Anna noticed, above the beak of his nose. That was part of the reason for the intensity of his expression. For a moment she even felt afraid of him.

Twenty minutes before the gallery was due to close, Thorn suddenly appeared by Anna's side.

"I've been looking for you," he said. "Have you been here long?"

"Only a few minutes." Close up, his size and beauty shattered her thoughts. She had never really kissed anyone, but she knew absolutely that she would kiss him. His shirt was blue, reflecting color into his eyes. She said, "I'm sorry . . . Pauline couldn't make it."

"Did you want your friend along?" He seemed surprised. "Then I'm afraid I'm the one who ought to apologize."

"Why?"

"I didn't invite her."

Heat rushed to Anna's face, she was terribly afraid she'd sneeze. She felt so overcharged with hope, and with the agonizing suspicion Thorn saw straight through all her pitiful maneuvering to be with him alone.

He began to walk with Anna, pointing out his favorite things. There were plenty of large, brightly glazed and colored figurines on display in the main gallery, where most of the people sipped wine or strolled about with brochures in their hands. But Thorn led her to side rooms to look at simple white or pale green vases in locked cabinets. The vases were really old, not Neo-Traditionalist.

Later, as they stood on the street outside the gallery, Anna confessed she'd never noticed pottery that way before.

"I guess with art I mainly look for the story, you know? Like if it's a picture, I think about what it's of. If it makes me feel what's going on in the story." Anna realized this was probably the stupidest possible thing to say. It revealed the abysmal depths of her immaturity.

"But that's the secret of Chinese art," Thorn told her. "It's pure form. A Sung vase stands alone in space, the way a perfect moment stands alone in time. Do you understand what I'm saying, I wonder."

This time Anna was careful and didn't answer.

He waited with her at her bus stop. They sat side by side on the bench, not touching at all.

He said, continuing his thought almost to himself, "A man might live a long life and not know more than two or three truly perfect moments."

"It doesn't matter," she asked, "what comes before or after?"

"Nothing comes before or after a perfect thing." Then he made a restless gesture, like brushing away something that clung to his face. "It's wrong for me to be here with you," he said.

"Why? You're not doing anything to hurt me."

"You haven't given me that power, yet. But you are very young, and I am . . . not so young."

She asked how old he was, and he answered twenty-nine. Possibly to spare Anna humiliation, he didn't ask her age.

She said, "I don't really see what difference age makes."

"Don't you?" A quick half-smile, half-grimace accompanied his question. "I wish I didn't."

Anna's bus lumbered up the street. She pointed it out, but he didn't seem to notice. He was looking at her with such intentness that she had to glance away. She fiddled with the hem of her skirt, pleating it between her fingers. She wished he'd ask her phone number, or even her last name, but he didn't.

She said, "I'm not really all that fragile, you know."

"Perhaps not. Perhaps you are even invulnerable. Like a poem that seems as fresh and perfect when I read it as when some Chinese scribe laid his inky fingers on it, eight hundred years ago."

Anna had to clutch the handrail on the steps getting into the bus, like some old lady with feeble knees.

The last thing Thorn said to her, "I have a desk in the room reserved for writers, at the main library downtown. Sometimes I'm there in the afternoons, around four."

She watched him out of sight from the rear window. People left behind at bus stops always looked lonely to Anna. But Thorn wasn't pathetic in his loneliness, like most people. He was a person used to standing apart.

That night Anna began her diary on a brand-new blank cassette. She meant to preserve every moment of her time with Thorn, so that later, if she really had to suffer, she could go back and remember how perfect and beautiful her love had been.

ECSTASY

Anna still hadn't changed out of her pajamas. A plate on the floor beside her bed held the curling crusts from a peanut-butter-and-nothing sandwich. She'd started to do a tarot reading, but got sidetracked trying to figure out how to play solitaire with the seventy-eight-card deck. Now the cards lay scattered over the bedspread.

She hadn't even brushed her teeth yet, and it was past two in the afternoon. Yesterday, she'd been still a virgin. Today, look at her, she was already a slut.

Anna raked together the cards, smoothed out her square of green silk, shuffled. She held the deck between her palms, breathing on it for a moment before she began to lay out a new reading.

She drew the chariot, reversed—decadent desires. That made her smile. The man in the chariot drove without reins, controlling two mysterious beasts by the force of his will. Right way up, the chariot would be a sign of self-mastery.

Next she got the knight of cups, but now he was upside down, too. All these cards were reversed. Like an idiot, she'd lined them all up one way to play solitaire. Now she was turning them over the wrong way.

Since the reading seemed hopelessly contaminated anyway, Anna cheated. She turned the deck around in her hand before drawing the next card. This one came right way up—but talk about diseased luck! She'd drawn the devil.

Anna turned the card round and round in her fingers. Obviously it was meant to remind you of the lovers. There were the same naked man and woman, only now they had horns on their heads and chains around their necks. In place of the angel, a leering bearded devil stretched his bat wings above them.

She flipped over the last four cards in a hurry to see her final outcome. *Oh my god, the nine of swords!*

And the stupid phone was ringing again. Pauline must be calling to find out why she hadn't come over. Anna seriously considered not answering. She knew for a fact Pauline would twist her tarot reading into a bunch of outrageous prophesies about Thorn. Not that it wasn't a boost to have Pauline so interested in her and Thorn. Even though the affair had to be kept secret, it still majorly enhanced Anna's status, at least with Pauline. Only, Pauline could be so insistent, and there were things . . . intimate things, doubts and desires . . . Anna didn't always want to share.

She frowned at the card she held. A woman in bed wept into her hands. Nine swords hung over her. Anna threw the card down and ran to catch the phone.

"Yeah, it's me."

A silence. Then, "Anna?"

"Thorn." His name was like a sweet taste dissolving on her tongue.

He asked how she was feeling. "Not sad at all? Not sore?"

"Only a tiny bit."

"You were such a virgin. Now you're blushing."

"No, really, I—I never blush. I don't get red in the sun, even. It's just how my skin is, like a vampire or something."

Anna slid down cross-legged on the kitchen floor, clutching the phone. She could smell her body, open, unwashed.

He asked, "When am I going to see you again?"

Anna told him about her plans with Pauline for the evening. The Caffè Mezzaluna—well, she knew that wasn't his favorite place, but the cousin was willing to drive there. The cousin had a license and ID . . . She began to notice the lengthening silence at the other end of the line.

Thorn said, gently, that he wasn't quite free that evening.

Anna felt like a puppy that's been caught with muddy paws on the sofa. Of course he wouldn't want to hang out with a bunch of stupid adolescents. This wasn't teen romance, for him. She'd been talking like they were going together, just because he'd slept with her.

Thorn was speaking about his own plans. He said the Pacific Writers' Retreat was hosting a reception for an old teacher of his, Rosemarie Barkis. Did Anna know her work?

Anna shook her head dumbly.

"I suppose she's more of an institution on the East Coast. Some of us will be going to dinner with her before the reception . . . I can't bring you, you know."

"Oh, I know," Anna said quickly.

Thorn said the reception would be open to the public, and Rosemarie would read. Anna could go to that.

"And your friend, if she likes. I should be able to drive you

home afterwards, though one of you will have to squeeze behind the seats."

Which proved that karma was true. Because she'd let go vol-
untarily of her desire, it had returned to her as a gift.

Still, Anna felt obliged to say, "I'm not sure a literary reception sounds like really Pauline's sort of thing. It would be bitchy
of me to stand her up . . ."

She wanted him to protest. She longed to hear him say that
it was only Anna he cared to see. But Thorn was too honorable
to persuade against her conscience. Anna had to argue herself
into the decision.

Though, come to think, the prospect of acting bitchy to
Pauline offered its own small subversive thrill. Of course,
Pauline would wring every last detail out of her on Monday, at
school. But for tonight, at least, Anna could hug her secrets to
herself. She opted to avoid conflict by blaming the no-show on
her mother. *Too bad, can't get out tonight. Talk to you later.* She
tried to keep joy from sounding in her voice.

"Please, everybody, find a seat—on the floor, if necessary!"
The woman pitched her announcement above the babble of
conversation filling the two main downstairs rooms of the Writers' Retreat House. Rosemarie Barkis would now read some
samples of her newest work. The woman set her fingertips together and gazed ceilingward to indicate the rapture they could
all expect.

From a place on the floor behind a flowered armchair Anna
couldn't see Thorn anymore. But she had seen him. He knew
she was there. For the time being at least, she felt content just
to hear the poems.

When she'd first arrived, Anna hadn't recognized anybody, not surprisingly. She'd spent a painful quarter hour in the entry hall, turning over leaflets about the Retreat House endowment fund, guest speakers, upcoming workshop sessions. It wasn't crowded enough for Anna to be just another warm body. People looked up from their conversations long enough to register surprise at her presence, her immaturity probably. Or at her mother's peacock-green velvet shirt, which she had borrowed and now recognized to be hideously garish.

Eventually Anna had acquired a cup of lukewarm punch and a post by the flowered armchair. From there she could see through an archway to what must have been the dining room of the original small bungalow-style house. She watched the guest of honor make her triumphal entry. She came from upstairs, where Anna now realized there must have been another gathering with more favored guests. They all came trooping down the stairs and took their places around a long conference table.

Rosemarie Barkis turned out to be a pleasant-looking fat black lady trailing yards of purple chiffon. Her thin gray hair was center-parted and glistened with oil above her forehead. In the back, it rose up like a cloud of steam.

Suddenly Anna recognized the man seating himself beside the poet. Sexy Dex—though he looked older, more serious and important than when she'd met him at the café. Then Thorn came in, carrying a microphone stand. He leaned over the table to adjust the mike for Rosemarie Barkis. He wore the cuffs of his shirt rolled back, exposing the long clean sinewy lines of his arms. A shock rushed through Anna, so for a moment she could barely see.

She stared fixedly at an Asian couple beside Thorn at the table. The woman had a pale flat face that reflected light like the moon. On second look, Anna decided she wasn't actually plain, only her features were incredibly delicate.

The woman noticed Anna staring. She adjusted one eyebrow like the feathered antenna of a moth. She leaned forward and said something to Thorn, who followed the direction of her eyes back to Anna. He raised his hand in a casual greeting, then turned back to the microphone.

Watching his profile, Anna had thought, it was there, in the high arch of his nose, the curl of his lip below—somehow precisely there lay the secret of his superiority over the whole race of mankind.

Now, as she sat on the floor, her view of him was blocked, so she leaned her head against the back of the armchair and closed her eyes. She'd met Thorn in the second week of August. Today was October 17. In all those weeks she'd been with him five times. Her life no longer flowed forward but staggered from meeting to meeting, with only desert spaces between. In his presence she'd felt frustrated by his caution; apart, she'd been tormented by fear that the whole affair was a figment of her imagination. But now everything had changed. Now they were actually lovers. Every polite public smile, every carefully nondescript gesture became a thrilling move in a game of forbidden love.

Rosemarie Barkis read her poems in a powerful deep voice. The poems surprised Anna. For such a cheerful-looking old lady, Rosemarie Barkis packed a load of rage. She especially seemed to hate every man she'd ever gone to bed with, and evidently there had been plenty.

Anna sipped her punch. She wondered if it might be mildly alcoholic. It tasted like canned iced tea.

When people stood up and moved around after the reading,

Anna stayed in her place. She knew without looking up that Thorn was coming toward her. She trembled a little from the effort of keeping perfectly still, because she knew he was watching.

He reached out his hand to help her up.

"I was afraid you'd gone home. I didn't see you here."

She smiled back politely. She felt astonished that the whole room full of people did not turn and stare at the dazzling messages that flashed in the air between them.

Thorn reintroduced Anna to David Dexter Fromm, and also to the Asian woman, who had a Chinese last name. Dex bowed over Anna's hand, so she saw a round dollar-sized bald spot in his bushy hair.

Dex asked Anna how she'd liked the reading. Now she had to be careful. She was launching her canoe on the swift race of sophisticated conversation. Thorn was listening. Anna answered that she thought the reading had been powerful. Her own voice sounded high-pitched and weenie. She ventured further and said the poems seemed a bit alike.

"I thought, maybe if she'd cut back on the outrage a little . . . I mean, they might've seemed, well, subtler."

"So, you think love poetry is an inappropriate vehicle for sexual politics?" said the Chinese woman. She wore a gray gown that clung like spiderweb. Up close, she seemed younger than Anna had thought, not much more than thirty. Anna felt obscurely threatened by her comment. She hadn't even realized it was supposed to be love poetry.

"No, Anna's right," said Thorn. "This new stuff of Barkis's lacks the finesse we saw in the *New Yorker Pieces.*"

Dex said, when were they going to see some love poems

from Thorn. Anna thought he was leering at her meaningfully. She sipped punch so as not to have to look at him. Maybe that was just his natural expression. He leered at his oatmeal in the morning, probably.

Thorn took the cup out of her hand. He smiled at the bite marks around the paper rim. "You need to be careful of this stuff," he said. "Dex mixed it, and it's lethal."

"Come on, Thorn," said Dex. "Just one little love lyric in your Chinese style, to round off my anthology. I don't get enough mannered pieces, it's all rage, like the girl says."

Thorn made a gesture like brushing flies away. He said everybody wanted love poems because they were short and there was no effort to understanding them.

"They're the fast food of literature. Seriously, I think half the time when people say the words *love* and *hate*, what they're talking about is actually food."

Dex raised his hands in mock surrender. "I love Polish sausage . . . an obscene confession, from a Jew."

"I adore you, darling, pass the ketchup," said the Chinese woman. Her laugh sent shimmers down the gray dress.

"But what a cynic you are, Thorn," Dex complained. "Where's your heart?"

"He hasn't got one," said the woman.

"You're the cynics," Thorn said. "I'm the one trying to talk about poetry, and you keep dragging in meat."

Because heart was meat, Thorn told them. People always needed to whack off their own piece of the carcass. Then, if they were civilized, they'd sugar it over with sentimentality and call that *love*. But they were just growling over sugared meat.

"Teriyaki love," Anna murmured, "with a stick through it."

Amazingly, they all laughed, as if she'd scored some brilliant conversational coup. Only Anna seemed to understand Thorn really meant what he'd been saying. Thorn despised food—and sleep—all the mundane comforts of life. If he were an animal he'd be a bird, some vast winged raptor at home in stony places.

"Are you having a dull evening?" Thorn asked quietly, under cover of the laughter. He touched the breast pocket of his shirt, an apparently random gesture, but enough to show her the white edge of a folded paper. Her own white onionskin bond. It was the poem she had sent to him two days ago, the day before they became lovers.

"It came this afternoon," he said. "A wonderful, unexpected gift. I would love to hear you read it to me."

Anna shook her head and turned to Dex, who was also speaking to her. She had no idea what Dex said. A welling up, like massive choirs of music, swelled her breast. She rose through the air on its silent outpouring. The chatter and the faces of the others faded to distance.

She'd been so afraid to show her poem to Thorn, that's why she'd mailed it. She wanted him to be her mentor, to work with her, not just to smile and say how good, like useless teachers at school. But she could never read aloud for him. She couldn't bear to see his face as he listened, like the face of God in judgment.

People were leaving the reception. The talk turned to cars: where did you leave yours, who's riding with whom.

"We have room for Anna, don't we?" Thorn said to the Chinese woman. "I don't want her taking the bus alone at night."

"No, of course not," cried Dex.

The woman said, what about Professor Ho.

Thorn laughed. "Jerry Ho is yearning for us to strand him so he'll have an excuse to go back with Rosemarie to her hotel."

"Brave man," murmured Dex.

Now Anna saw how she'd been caught out by her own stupid racist assumption, that two Asian people sitting together must make a couple. With a sensation of tumbling through empty space, Anna began to understand who this slinky woman must be. Thorn had actually said her name earlier, but Anna had been too lost in space to recognize it—Elaine Song. The Song Gallery must belong to her. She was Thorn's ex-fiancée.

Elaine drove. Thorn sat beside her in the front seat, with Anna and Dex in back. Dex stretched his arm across the top of the seat. His fingers rested by Anna's cheek—black hairs sprouting round a heavy gold ring. First she met the queen of swords, and now here was the devil spreading his bat wings.

Elaine didn't drive Anna all the way home to Westview. She stopped at Thorn's building, where he'd left his own car, an almost-vintage 1967 sports car. They all went upstairs to Thorn's apartment. On the way inside, Anna paused to touch the white card tacked beside Thorn's buzzer. *TA and ES*, it said simply.

TA and ES. So. Anna was not like some grade-school girl with a crush, going around scribbling his initials all over her binder. She understood Thorn was a grown man, while she was still officially a child. Immense barriers of time and space lay between them—her school years, his career in New York—they might never come together as independent adults. She rubbed her thumb over the white card. Maybe if it looked dirty he'd get around to taking it down.

Thorn's apartment didn't run to much furniture. There might once have been more that had belonged to Elaine, but Thorn despised clutter. Dex took the only good chair. Elaine bustled around in the kitchen, opening wine. Thorn perched on the edge of his desk. Anna curled up on a corner of the futon to wait until Thorn could drive her home.

She didn't take part in the conversation, which was mostly about a book that Dex wanted to put out, an anthology of new poets. Thorn would be in it, of course. And Dex wanted him to persuade Rosemarie Barkis to write an introduction, because she "represented an established voice," which could be seen as "handing down the torch." His voice went on and on, punctuated by his yapping laugh.

Anna drank the wine Elaine handed her. Dex refilled her glass, at least once.

"Stop that, Dex," Elaine said. "You'll make the poor girl silly."

Defiantly, Anna drank off the glass. She didn't actually like wine, so normally she wouldn't have. But she wasn't at all drunk. On the contrary, she felt so alert her skin practically tingled with awareness.

Though her foot was going to sleep. Anna stroked her leg experimentally. Pins and needles followed the line of her touch. By stroking very, very lightly she could bring the tingle up to the surface. Or even just above the surface of her skin, like a static buzz.

I'm hypnotizing myself, Anna thought. *I'm floating.*

It was a kind of dead man's float. The conversation washed over her head. Underwater voices boomed in her ears.

"I think she's gone to sleep." Elaine's voice came from somewhere distant.

Anna heard the clink as Elaine picked up glasses. She sensed Thorn was standing over her.

He said, "I think she's just pretending to sleep, so we'll talk about her."

Anna tried to protest, but found she couldn't separate her lips . . . or her eyelids.

Dex said, "Look how she curls her toes. Like a baby."

"She's quite exquisite," Elaine said. "But how old is she, really?"

"Almost sixteen," said Thorn.

"You fucking crazy man," Dex said. "You could get your ass nailed for this! I thought she was at least—well—"

"Seventeen?" Thorn laughed.

"I just hope to god you're being careful. I mean, you're using . . . well, protection?"

"Don't be vulgar, Dex. Of course I'm looking after her. She's very special. This is not a Lolita story."

Elaine said she was going to get her coat. Anna drifted into a dream where Dex and Elaine and Thorn tiptoed round and round, like witches in *Macbeth*.

Dex was saying, "I don't know that I admire everything about you, Thorn, but I do envy your luck."

"You admire my work."

"That, too."

Anna felt Thorn's weight beside her on the futon. The room was dark, but he'd lit one candle and placed it on the floor.

"I think you drank too much wine," he said. He stroked the velvet of her sleeve. The smooth inside slithered on her arm.

She struggled to sit up. "Did they leave?"

"Yes. But I can't take you home like this. You'd better stay awhile."

"I'm sorry."

"Don't be."

The velvet slid off her shoulders. It seemed to Anna in her waking dream that her whole outer self husked away, leaving her bodiless as the candlelight. She raised her arms like white flames. He kissed them, kissed the hollow between her breasts. Through blurred lashes she saw light polishing his hair, his naked shoulders. His hands stroked traces of fire down her sides, across her belly. She was like a white paper that catches fire. She arched and curled. A roar like burning filled her ears.

Afterwards she really did fall asleep. She woke to see him lying with his head propped on one hand, watching her. His other hand rested, heavy and warm, at the angle of her waist.

"It's late," he said. "I'm afraid your mother will be worrying why you're not home."

"She won't even notice. She never worries, because I've always been so good."

She saw his teeth gleam. "You're still good."

"That's not what I meant!"

"That's not what I meant, either. Though it's true." His fingers began to explore the lines of her ribs. "What did you think of Elaine?"

"She's . . . very beautiful."

"Not everybody sees that. But I knew you would."

"She made me think of those Chinese vases . . . the plain green ones in the gallery."

"She wanted to meet you. Did you mind?"

"Not really," she said, carefully.

"Anna . . . I don't want to hide things. What I'm like. If I can't be good, like you—at least I won't be petty."

After another minute he said, "Your skin feels cool. Should I get a blanket?"

But she didn't feel cold. His hand gliding down her thigh was enough.

He said, "What would it take, I wonder, to make you sweat . . . to make you turn red and blunder, like other women?"

"Why would you want me to?" she asked.

He cast her a bright sideways glance, a half smile. "Men always long to spoil what's perfect," he said. "Didn't you know that?"

FOLLY

Sunday passed in a daze. Anna went through motions. Homework. Load of laundry. Dishes . . . She found herself adding grace steps between the dishwasher and the plate cupboard—bend, raise two cups, pivot and glide—Anna moved through a stately dance with her imagined lover.

She remembered there was a myth, a Greek myth about a girl . . . The god Zeus made love to her in the form of a shower of gold. Anna stood with the cups raised above her head and imagined the gold raining over her, striking her skin to numbness, bearing her down. Afterwards the girl must have lain faint and heavy, the coins scattered round her, their weight cooling on her thighs.

On Monday morning Anna woke up feeling like moldy death. Groaning pathetically, she groped her way to the bathroom, then to the kitchen, where her mother stood holding up a coffee pot like some perky housewife out of fifties TV.

Her mother said, "Why is it the one day I take time off to make a proper breakfast, you won't eat?"

Actually, her mother had taken the morning off work to

go shopping with Anna's sister, for last-minute wedding stuff.

"Why can't Rennie pick her own stuff? It's her wedding," said Anna.

"Because I'm paying for it, is why."

Anna announced she was going back to bed for a while. "I've got some kind of stomach thing. Anyway, I won't miss anything important before geometry third period."

"Just be sure you keep your grades up," her mother said unsympathetically.

"My grades are up! When did I ever get bad grades?"

"I'm only warning you. Especially if you're serious about this writing business, Anna. You'd better make darn sure you get the right education."

"Oh, you mean an MBA, like Vonda?"

"Absolutely, like Vonda. Or do you want to be a free spirit like Rennie, live in a slum and work at Pancake House? Trust me, even poets have to pay the rent. And you'll have a lot more energy left over for your hobbies if you're not hauling trays ten hours a day—"

Shrieking soundlessly, Anna fled back to her room.

She curled up on her bed. *Like a grub in an apple*, Anna thought. It seemed a fitting metaphor for her entire life, she was dreaming she'd mutate to some winged creature, but meanwhile her universe amounted to a mere series of sensations passing through her inert body. Hormone surges. Gut reactions. Anna moaned and clutched her stomach.

Then a long session on the toilet brought glorious relief. How ignoble, that's all it took to change her whole philosophy of life. She wished Thorn had E-mail so she could send him a message. But Thorn wrote everything out longhand with his gold-tipped pen. Come to think, this was hardly the sort of insight she could share, anyway.

Anna pulled on jeans and a soft flannel shirt. She walked down the hill to the bus stop with her jacket open, so the damp wind flapped it out behind. She'd missed the yellow peril but flagged a regular Metro bus.

She thought if it weren't for a possible quiz in geometry she might be tempted to ditch this morning, go into the wilderness park beside the river. From her bus window she could see jogging trails disappearing into the trees. She felt light and empty inside as a blown eggshell. *Screw geometry.*

The bus left her off by the highway sign for the Grace Petrie Memorial Park. From there she had a half-mile hike to the main parking lot, where there were picnic tables and toilets and a reader board showing the trails. Even this early on a wet morning she saw a few cars in the lot. Anna stashed her backpack behind the women's restroom.

Probably she'd better monitor phone messages for a few days, in case someone from the office called. She'd never actually done this before, just skipped school without any excuse. Other people talked about ditching all the time, like it was really no big thing. Pauline's friends talked that way.

At the beginning of school in September, Anna had steeled herself to face Pauline's group, maybe even eat lunch with them, though she was a lowly sophomore and they were juniors, like Pauline. She'd gone so far as to rehearse a few casual witticisms on the tape recorder. Her preparations turned out irrelevant since none of those people ever listened to each other, anyway. Maybe if she'd been talking about Thorn . . . After a few weeks Anna had gratefully faded from their lunchtime scene.

She chose a broad paved trail with a gentle slope heading down to the river. To her dismay, she soon heard voices and pounding feet coming uphill toward her. *Some kind of group run*, Anna thought.

She turned off the paved way where a barely visible track plunged much more steeply downhill. And only just in time, she realized, as Westview High team colors flashed by above her. She hoped this new trail wouldn't fade out in the middle of some blackberry jungle.

Dripping alders closed over her head. Their pale moss-stained trunks crowded the path or lay broken and sprouting ferns across it. The air smelled rich and full of rotting vegetation.

The track degraded into a rocky gully veined with running water. Anna's shoe sank into mud. She wrenched it out, staggered through a screen of tattered maple saplings—then stopped, clutching at an angled branch.

The whole slope had sloughed away below her, leaving raw red clay and bare roots dangling. Anna wedged her feet sideways. Water oozed around her rubber soles.

Twenty feet below, the slope ended in a rubble field of boulders and broken trees washed up by last winter's floods. Scrubby plants grew up between the cracks. Beyond this wasteland the river flowed broad and smooth and brown, pockmarked with hidden currents.

A man stood on the hard-packed beach. Anna wondered what he'd gone down there to do. Maybe there was a dog playing somewhere out of sight, beside the water.

Maybe he wondered about her, too. He turned and seemed to watch as she worked around the edge of the slough. She clung to plants, slid on her butt, jumped the last few feet, and landed painfully on her knees in a patch of gravel.

From there she couldn't see the man anymore. Which was just as well, you never knew how much other people would notice or care if you were breaking the rules, like ditching school.

Anna picked her way over rocks and logs to the beach, to the edge of the water, over the edge. The bright current rippled around her shoes. Funny how the water never looked brown, close up. For an instant her shoes seemed made of silver. Then they were soaked.

Not far from here, some poor little kid got drowned on Labor Day weekend. That was over on the River City side, near the marina. They were always posting warnings to people not to swim in this river, not to eat the fish . . . Though judging from the wads of old fishing line spiderwebbed over the rocks, there were plenty who did.

There was that man again, climbing across a jumble of big boulders that thrust out into the water. Oddly, he kept his hands in the pockets of his coat, only taking one out to steady his balance occasionally. Anna saw there was no dog.

She smiled at him vaguely. That turned out to be a big mistake. The man began to move purposefully toward her.

Anna made a show of checking her watch. "Uh-oh, I'm late," she said.

She walked briskly back up the beach. As she passed in front of the man, she nodded curtly, no eye contact, cutting off further communication.

Without appearing to notice her at all, the man shifted direction so he was trailing behind her.

Anna walked faster. Why didn't he say something to her, if that's what he wanted? Her heart began to pump uncomfortably. Obviously, there would be no going back the way she'd come down the slope. Where did all the proper trails come out? Or did she really want to risk meeting up with this man, somewhere on a trail among the shadows of the trees?

She looked and saw him only a few yards back, stooping to clamber over a rock. She called, "Are you following me?"

Still crouching, the man glanced up, but his eyes wouldn't meet hers. It was as if he were blind, and merely turned toward the sound of her voice. Anna noticed he was wearing polished businessman's loafers, the kind with little leather tassels.

She began to run, cutting across the rough ground, jumping from rock to rock. She was wearing better shoes than he was for this type of action. A minute later she saw him give up and turn away, toward the trees. Soon she lost sight of him completely.

She followed fishermen's trails littered with ancient beer cans through scrub thickets and alongside the water. She came to a place where a stream etched its channel across the sand. So she couldn't go any farther this way, unless she wanted to wade up to her waist in frigid water. It was lucky that man hadn't known he could cut her off here, or she might really have been in trouble.

She followed the stream back toward the woods. A huge old fir had ripped off the face of the cliff and tumbled partway across the stream bed. Mosses and ferns dripped from the tree's spongy sides. The flat mass of the roots, still clotted with earth, stood up, forming almost a little cave. Anna followed it around, under the shadow of the hillside. And came face to face with the man.

Anna stepped backward. Unspoken words flashed across her brain. *Please. Oh no.*

The man stepped forward. His hands came out of his pockets. His tongue came out of his mouth. It flickered across his lips that looked so dry . . . tiny dry gullies all around them.

Anna stumbled out of the shade behind the roots. She looked frantically which way she should run—and saw somebody else. A guy not much older than herself stood up on the fallen tree trunk, looking down at her. Where had he come from so suddenly? The woods, most likely, since she would've seen him on the beach.

She called out to him. "Hi!"

He said *Hi* back. His eyes registered the man behind her.

She wanted to scream at him, *Help me.* What she said was, "I'm sorry I'm late."

"No big thing. I just got here myself. You want a hand up?" He went down on one knee and held out his hand to help Anna onto the tree.

Together they looked down at the man. His hands were back in his coat pockets. He stared at them in his weird blind way, then turned and began to trudge slowly up the beach. Every now and again he flapped his elbows or flung out one hand to keep from stumbling.

"I hope he falls and cracks his nose on a rock!" Anna said.

"I broke my nose once. Skateboard . . . It hurt a lot more than I expected."

"Obviously, then, it was a failed experiment."

They both laughed. The sound made the man glance back over his shoulder.

The boy said maybe they should go somewhere. "If you want."

"Where?" asked Anna. She was trying not to look at his nose, not that there seemed anything much wrong with it.

"I don't know. How about . . . to the end of this log?"

He led the way. Anna decided she liked the way he walked—loose-boned, like a dancing skeleton. Otherwise, there was nothing particularly memorable about his looks: coloring, between blond and brown; build, tall and bony; the usual numbers of eyes, ears, teeth. He wore baggy pants, a sweatshirt, shoes but no socks. From the back his hair looked like he'd cut it himself, using toenail clippers.

They came to the narrow end of the tree. Its top had lodged in a bank about eight feet above some greenish mudflats. So they turned around and walked back.

Anna told about ditching classes and getting followed by that man. The guy said he'd walk up to the parking lot with her, if she wanted.

"You know the way?" she asked.

"Sure. There's a blacktop trail comes out just behind that bunch of bushes."

"Now you tell me!"

"Well, I thought we ought to let that sucker get a head start." He laughed. "For a minute there, I was afraid he was going to blow us both away."

"With what?" said Anna.

"What do you think? He was packing, didn't you see?"

Anna said she didn't believe it.

"Well, you got to figure," he said. "The guy keeps his right hand in his pocket the whole time. There's only two things likely to be that important. In this case I thought the bulge looked pretty far to the side . . . Hey! Hey, I'm sorry if I upset you."

Anna slid off the tree. Her knees buckled as she hit the dirt. She bent her head between them, feeling queasy.

"It's not *you* who upset me."

He sat down on the trunk above her. "What's your name?" he asked.

"Anna Pavelka. What's yours?"

"My name . . ." He made a gesture like a magician plucking a bouquet out of the air for her. "My name is Thomas Dylan."

"Oh, like the poet!" said Anna. "Only backwards."

He flung out his arms, then toppled backwards until he hung by his knees from the tree. His head dangled just above her shoulder.

"Or upside down?" he asked.

"The fool reversed!" she cried.

He clutched at his already chaotic hair. "How do you know everything about me?"

"It's my sign, I think, the fool reversed. I get him every time."

He didn't say, *What are you talking about*, as most people would. He said, "At your service, my lady."

By the time they reached the parking lot, it was almost noon. A lunchtime crowd of people with large dogs or small children had showed up to romp on the battered grass beyond the picnic tables. Any delusions Anna might have nurtured about making it back to school in time for geometry died quietly, and un-mourned.

She retrieved her backpack and carried it back to the park-ing lot, where she found Thomas Dylan standing beside an im-mense old banana-colored American car.

He spread out his arms in a gesture of modest pride. "You are looking at a man who possesses his own automobile."

"Cool," said Anna.

"Yeah. She's got a 351 Windsor . . . dual catalytics . . . 226 rear end. This girl's a cruiser. She used to be with a police detective up in Hoquiam or some damn place. Look here, see where the spotlight used to go?" His fingers lovingly traced some rusted-out bolt holes by the driver's window. "I think he ran her into a deer. One of these days, though, I swear I'm going to get me one of those little cheap blue Mexican glasses—you know, like they put candles in?—and glue it on the dashboard, here . . ."

He opened the door to show Anna the place where he would fix his fake police flasher. Anna noticed he had little crinkles, almost like dimples, at the corners of his eyes. They deepened when he laughed.

"So, where do you want to go?" he said, still holding the car door open.

"Wait a minute, I can't just go off someplace in a car with a total stranger! I don't know anything about you."

"What do you want to know?"

What did she want to know, besides that he had a cheerful temper and nothing else to do? "Tell me where you live," she said. "Do you go to school? Anything!"

He said, "I live in River City, 2397 Mondago Avenue, behind the Pizza Hut. With my mom, name of Charlene. I got ID, you want to see—? No, you don't care about that. So, what else? I used to board a lot, till I got involved with Nicole Ford—that's what I call her. Now I'm a reformed character, got to have a job so I can pay for gas. I don't smoke, drink, or do drugs unless somebody gives me a hit for free. That good enough for you?"

"Not so fast! Tell me . . . what job? And what about school?"

"Oh, I just deliver pizza. I go to River City High, which sucks sewage . . . No, seriously, I don't mind school. I pretty much pass most stuff. I might even graduate this year."

Anna felt silly keeping up the inquisition. She was just interested. She asked him what he thought he'd do after graduating, go to college? But he said he probably couldn't get in any place but community college. Maybe someday he'd do that, boost his grades so he could really go somewhere, a big university somewhere.

"But I don't know. Two years at Community seems like a long time to hang around, waiting."

"So what else would you do, if you didn't go there?"

"Hang around, I guess." He laughed. "Like my mom's always telling me, whichever way I cast my gaze, brilliant prospects lie before me."

Anna said, "We could go someplace for a coffee, I guess."

That evening Anna took out her tape recorder and taped an entry about Thomas Dylan.

> *But I kept on wanting to call him Dylan, because of Dylan Thomas. He said he didn't mind . . . We wound up going to the Veterans' Thrift Store and picking buttons out of this huge box they had, all full of buttons. We made up rules for them, like each one stood for some secret message. This big blue one meant,* Everything you say means exactly the opposite. *And a brass Army one with an eagle on it meant,* Fly! The person before you is your secret mortal enemy. *Dylan flashed it at me while I was trying to pay for coffee at this place we went to over in River City. I had to crawl under the table and pretend like I'd dropped my quarter . . .*

Anna smiled to herself, remembering. But she felt grateful she'd never have to go back to that place and face the beady-eyed waitress.

"This is a dive, but they have great rolls," Dylan had told her when he took her in there. "You order soup or something and they'll bring a bunch of rolls. I can make myself a pickle sandwich, that way we'll both get enough."

They'd only had about four dollars between them, minus what the buttons cost.

Watching him eat his disgusting sandwich, Anna had asked, "What are you so happy about?"

"Me?" Dylan grinned through a mouthful of ketchup. "I'm in love."

This was interesting. "Does she love you?" Anna asked.

"I don't know, but she will."

"How do you know?"

"Because. If she didn't I'd be miserable, and right now I feel like nothing bad is going to happen to me, my whole *life*, man. Like God must like me better than other people."

Anna looked at him in wonder. She said, "I love somebody, too. A man . . . His name is Thorn. Thorn Arneson. He's older than me. I don't get to be with him as often as I want. There's times I feel like love makes me miserable as much as happy."

"Tell me about it."

It had taken her a minute to realize he really meant *tell him*, not just an expression.

"I don't always feel like that, of course," she said, defending Thorn.

"No, of course not."

But she could see by his expression he understood how she meant. It made her feel a little weird about him right at first, like he might be one of those guidance counselor-type people, switching instantly from happy to serious to empathize with whatever you said. To change the subject, she asked what was his girlfriend's name.

He was mashing the rest of his roll into soggy pills. "Her name? Oh, Nicole."

That made her laugh. "Nicole! I thought, when you said before . . . Like you said you got together with Nicole? I thought you meant the car! Like, you kept calling the car *she*."

"Why would you think that?" he said. "Nicole's a girl, just like you."

Anna's mother tapped on her door, then stuck her head in. "Phone's for you."

Anna hastily dropped a pillow over the tape recorder. "Did . . . did you ask who it was?"

"He said to tell you Dylan."

"Oh. O.K. I can plug my phone in here."

And though she'd wished it would be Thorn, Anna found she wasn't desperately disappointed. It was something just to have a person she could talk to occasionally about him . . . Somebody (not like Pauline) who was in love himself, so he might understand the weird things you might do or think. The way love made you feel, all taken apart and the pieces put back weirdly.

THE LOVERS

Anna's father was Larry Pavelka. Larry had lived all over the country working different jobs, or sometimes no job. But what the hell, he'd say, he never cared for the daily grind, the bird in the hand. The sky was full of birds.

One time when Anna was little she'd asked him, "Daddy, are you a businessman?"

"I'm a self-made man," he'd told her.

Anna had liked the sound of that. "Does it mean you're magic?"

"It means anything I damn well want. That's the beauty of it, don't you see?"

Then he'd tossed her twice, three times, straight into the sky, till her head turned giddy and his laughter flew up around her like champagne bubbles.

Anna was drinking champagne now because it was Rennie's wedding. She sat at a table beside the Riverside Inn Conference Facility #2 dance floor. Couples shuffled around to the kind of tunes rented guys in blue tuxedos play.

A passing waiter refilled Anna's glass, since she was holding it up. Actually, she couldn't put the annoying thing down. This so-called glass was plastic, manufactured in two parts, the cup with a pointy stem and a base for the stem to fit into. Anna's base had fallen off and rolled away somewhere under the table.

Across from Anna, two old ladies whispered together behind hands knobby with arthritis and rings.

The plump one, bobbing her head, said, "You can certainly see where those Pavelka girls get their looks."

Her eyes were on Anna's father dancing with some girlfriend of Rennie's, his sleek dark head laid against her sugar-frosted curls. He spun the girl around suddenly, and she let out a squeak like a bathtub toy.

Anna and Vonda got their looks from Larry. They had the same limp hair and drowned complexions. Wells of shadow under their eyes. But Rennie was a redhead with freckles on her arms and even across the tops of her round pink knees. Popsicle legs, Vonda used to call Rennie.

She means where we get our morals, Anna thought.

The old lady fixed Anna with a bright questioning look. She wore girlish-pink lipstick. Under her chins the silver ribbons of a corsage trembled. She asked, didn't Anna like her cake?

"She's saving it to put under her pillow," said her friend.

The friend was a dried-up kind of old person. Deep grooves ran down her cheeks. Her fingernails—even the skin of her fingers was stained deep nicotine yellow.

"Oh my yes," agreed the plump lady. "When we were girls, they used to wrap up tiny slices in silver netting and pass them out like party favors. To slip under our pillows."

"Why," said Anna.

"So we'd dream of our future husbands!" The dry lady had a short-breathed laugh like a dog panting in the heat.

The corsage lady said of course they didn't use to put all this cream and jam or what have you in the cake.

"No, it was just plain cake. Built to last, I guess you'd say."

The two ladies exchanged significant looks and nods.

"Excuse me," said Anna. She stood up, still clutching the champagne glass as if she meant to propose a toast.

The two ladies leaned forward with their bright, irrelevant smiles. How could they bear to do that, Anna wondered, mashing their boobs against the table edge? Didn't people feel their bodies any more, when they got old and squashy?

A memory of Thorn washed over her. Thorn's hand, heavy at her waist . . . then his thumb stroking along the curve of her stomach beneath her ribs. Like a wave drawn down the beach Anna felt her legs turning to water, draining away. She reached out and stabbed the point of her glass into the wedge of cake left on her plate.

A warm hand cupped her elbow.

"You all right, sweetheart?" It was the wedding photographer. "Pretty dress," he said soothingly.

"It's a grotesque dress," said Anna. She formed her lips around the words with care, like someone wrapping an odd-shaped package.

The bridesmaids' dresses were vast inverted bowls of chiffon in pale sherbet colors. Anna's was peach. It had a ruched bodice that puffed out as if stuffed with actual fruit. Vonda looked sallow and poisonous in lime-green. The thought occurred to Anna that these dresses could be Rennie's revenge for growing up wedged between two sisters who were naturally thin. But Rennie was too nice to think like that. She was the only actually nice person in their family.

The photographer steered Anna between couples on the

dance floor. Not that there were really all that many. Anna's mother had bought a special wedding-package deal that included the conference hall, but it was more space than they needed. Beyond the band stage and the brightly lit dance floor, the edges of the room grew shadowy. Most of the tables at the back had no chairs.

Outside the hotel on the highway a marquee proclaimed: WELCOME RENEE AND DAVE'S WEDDING GUESTS/SOUTH COUNTY BOOSTERS BANQUET.

"Where are you taking me?" Anna asked the photographer.

"We need to get all you bridesmaids together for an informal shot—"

"We already did that."

"That was a formal portrait. Now we're staging the informal groupings."

The photographer skipped around like a trained flea, setting up his shots. He started with some mother/daughter "combos."

"That's right, put your arm around the bride, Mommy. Heads together, now!"

Rennie laid her loose coppery curls against her mother's iron reinforced ones. Rennie looked as if she'd styled her hair by rolling down a hill; the effect was highlighted by some randomly inserted daisies. Her mother stuck out her tongue to dislodge a petal clinging to her lipstick.

Next came the wedding party. Rennie and Dave posed informally in the center, flanked by Anna with Rennie's ex-roommate on the left, and Vonda with Kev the best man on the right. Dave kept goofing around. He held out his wrists to Kev, who slapped a pair of party-gag handcuffs onto them. Then they all had to wait forever while Kev searched the pockets of his rented suit for the key.

Rennie's smile began to make tight little creases at the corners of her mouth, like quotation marks. Like you put quotation marks around some things to show you don't really mean them.

"Come on, everybody," chirped the photographer, "bright smiles, now! Let's really strut our stuff."

Anna wondered how much more of their stuff she could endure.

Vonda hissed at Kev, *"Get your hand off my ass."* In a lull of the dance music her voice crackled like a loudspeaker announcement.

Anna said she needed to use the bathroom. She set off blindly across the dance floor and bumped into her father.

He slipped a steadying arm around her waist. "Dance with me, Princess."

Anna leaned against her father's chest and let him rock her gently to the music.

"Are those tears I saw?" His fingers traced a line down her cheek. "Don't you know it's only us old fogies allowed to cry at weddings?"

"I can't believe Rennie's married to that—that—" Anna's shoulders jerked. "If Dave had red hair, you could pass him off for an orangutan. He wouldn't even need to get a job, he could get endangered-species funding."

Larry's laughter warmed the top of her head. Holding her arm out straight and stiff, he sailed her round and round the shining floor.

After their dance, he took Anna over to the buffet table and piled glistening shrimp onto a cup of shaved ice for her.

"Don't forget the lemon," Anna told him.

"Lemon it is." He used silver-plated tongs to crown her shrimp with lemon slices.

"Now an olive."

The olive rolled off the top.

"Dave's not so bad," said Larry. "No, really. I've been talking with him. He's not as stupid as he acts."

"*Look* at him," Anna cried. "He's humiliating Rennie. He doesn't even love her."

Dave was posing as a drunk for the photographer. He had one arm crooked around Rennie's neck, like the lamppost, while he chugged champagne out of a bottle.

"No. Well . . ." Larry sighed. "He can't, really. Renata gives him everything he wants before he has to love her."

Anna looked carefully at her father, at his thin face and expressive eyebrows, his hair just brushed with silver at the temples. He could be some distinguished actor or professor, instead of, currently, a manufactured-homes salesman in Pocatello, Idaho. Anna's mother had given him three children and twenty-one years of her life. What could she possibly have kept back, so that he might still love her?

Anna left Larry standing by the buffet table and went in search of her mother. She found her sitting at a table with "Joe and Louise," who were Dave's father and most recent stepmother.

Dave's father really did look like an orangutan. He had that pouchy fold of fat around his cheeks and under his chin that's supposed to make big male apes appear impressive. Louise was twenty years younger.

The other person at the table was a guy named Walt Durban, who worked at Anna's mother's office. Looking at Walt's shiny forehead and puffball stomach, Anna couldn't believe he was actually her mother's date, no matter what Vonda had told her.

There had been a while after the divorce when Anna's mother had dated different men, even brought some home to meet the girls and stay for weekends. Anna's favorite had been the last one, a guy named Danny who told jokes and used to let her stand on the toes of his steel-capped construction worker's boots. Anna had been too young to get told anything, but she remembered the yelling and stomping around, then the three days when Danny's car was left parked outside their building with all his stuff piled in the back seat. Vonda said Danny had been coming on to Rennie.

Nowdays Vonda said their mother was getting it off with somebody at work. *I mean, she's certainly there enough. Every time I call home, you tell me she's at the office—*

Vonda lived in New York, where she'd found her spiritual niche working as a fraudulent-claims investigator for Safcor Assurance.

"Hiya, howza girl?" Walt Durban hailed Anna.

"Would it be all right if I go home now?" Anna asked her mother.

"No, of course it's not all right! We have to stay at least until Rennie and Dave take off, and I get a chance to speak with the caterers."

"Looks like those boys're planning to make an all-nighter of it," said Dave's father, Joe.

"At least until Rennie tosses her bouquet, then."

"Or her bridegroom tosses his cookies," said Louise, sweetly.

"I could take the bus," said Anna.

"No, you could *not.* Anna, what's the matter with you?"

"Maybe I'm a little sick today."

Dave's father winked disgustingly at Walt Durban. "Lot of us going to feel that way in the morning, young lady."

"Oh, Lord!" said Anna's mother, raking stiff fingers through her hair. Halfway through, she realized what she was doing and reversed the gesture carefully, fluffing her curls back into place.

"Look," she said, and waved her hand, still stiff-fingered, at the reception hall. Maybe she meant to zap everyone with lightning. "I paid for all this. Why am I the only one not allowed to drink and act stupid?"

"I thought Dad was paying half," said Anna.

Her mother breathed out a sharp *ha*!

"It is traditional for the father of the bride to pay for the wedding," remarked Walt Durban, addressing the ceiling tiles.

"Thank you for your input," said Anna's mother. She told Anna there was a couch in the ladies' lounge. "Come on, you can lie down there. You'll feel better after a little while."

In the ladies' lounge Anna's mother took out a comb and began to pick at her hair.

"I need to find the best man and get the keys from him for the rental car," she said. "Somebody'll have to drive Dave to pick up his luggage . . ."

"He can drive himself," said Anna, on the couch.

"Not if we want him to live until tomorrow."

"If," said Anna.

"Listen, Anna," said her mother, "you can't judge a man by how he acts at a party. It's like feeding chocolate to a dog, or"—she jerked at the comb—"ouch! Apples to cows. Some men can't behave at parties. I remember at my wedding . . ." She put the comb away and took out her lipstick. "Larry had to have two best men, one on each side, to prop him up. Army buddies . . ." She smiled brightly, experimentally, at the mirror.

"They all had to be back at Fort Lewis by noon the next day. They were flying them out . . ."

"To Vietnam?" asked Anna.

"Mmm." Anna's mother came to sit beside her, at the edge of the ladies-room couch.

"Anna . . . let me tell you something. When you marry, be sure you marry for love. That way, afterwards . . ."

"What?" said Anna.

Her mother gave her the smile she'd practiced for the mirror. "Afterwards, at least you'll be able to remember why you did it."

Anna's mother went in search of Dave's best man. Anna sat alone on the couch, twisting up fistfuls of peach chiffon. All this—the love and promises and floaty dresses, that row of yawning toilet stalls, the old ladies gloating over their portions of cake—everything was so unbearably sordid. Not the champagne, the wedding itself made Anna sick.

Eventually she got up and sloshed cold water over her face. Outside the ladies' lounge she'd noticed a telephone alcove.

Thorn answered after seven rings. Then she almost let him hang up again without speaking, because her voice caught in her throat.

"It's me, Anna," she whispered.

"Anna! I thought you'd gone to a wedding. I pictured you there, surrounded by roses."

"Well, dyed-pink daisies, actually." Anna laughed. She relaxed her grip on the receiver.

"I can barely hear you. Wait a minute." He had music playing in the background, jazz guitar. Then he must have muffled the phone because the sound went dull, though she thought he was still speaking.

"I'm sorry," she began, "I just wanted to—"

"Someone else is here," he said.

Anna held her breath.

"Now I'm wishing you could be here with us. Would you like to?"

His voice was warm and gently teasing. But Anna flipped into panic mode. "No, that's impossible, I have to stay here, it's my sister's wedding!" She shouldn't have called, shouldn't have tried to force herself into his life. He would think she was a hysterical adolescent, checking up on him. Trying to own him.

She heard a woman's voice, questioning. Thorn answered off the phone, *It's Anna.*

Anna said, "Listen, I have to go now. Goodbye."

She hung up quickly and quietly, then stood leaning with her whole weight on the receiver, because she couldn't breathe, *couldn't bear*— She must be the stupidest person in the universe.

Why should she feel betrayed? Thorn had never pretended she was the only one. She'd never imagined he might marry her, or anything stupid like that. She'd tried to avoid imagining the future at all.

Because what had she to offer him—*an exchange of hearts,* like the rent-a-minister had said during the ceremony to Rennie and Dave? If Thorn were here she'd rip hers out and offer it to him, a smoking human sacrifice. And it would be a free gift, more real than wedding trash, china and Cuisinart, rings and vows. When she got home she'd say all this on the tape recorder. Because now she truly understood love and suffering, she would say it right.

When she got home. Suddenly the need to be home, in her own room, filled her with such yearning she couldn't stay here another ten minutes or she'd shrivel and die.

Anna picked up the phone again. This time she rang Dylan's number. He lived right near the Riverside Inn. He promised to pick her up out front, in his car.

"When? How soon can you get here?"

"Five minutes? Eight, to be on the safe side. Is that good enough?"

The chiffon dress hissed as Anna slid across the front seat of Dylan's big old Ford.

"You should've seen all these dresses stuffed into my mother's Neon," she told him. "Listen, I'm incredibly grateful for this. I didn't mean to, like, highjack you. I didn't even ask if you were doing something else, like with Nicole . . . ?"

Dylan said no problem, Nicole had a practice tonight for her Christmas recital.

Nicole was a dancer. She really got serious about it, practiced for hours every day and attended special evening classes because she missed so much school. Dylan had told Anna he thought Nicole did care about him, but he could never be number one with her. The dancing came first. Anna knew sometimes he felt pretty down, though he always denied it.

Anna said, "Christmas already! We haven't even had Thanksgiving."

"Yeah. Then she's going down to California to stay with her relatives over Christmas break."

Anna made sympathetic noises. Dylan said, did she want to ride around a little, go to the park or something? Anything she wanted, he was free.

Anna said probably better not. Her mother would call home as soon as she realized Anna wasn't at the hotel.

"I don't want her to worry. I don't know what got into me, really, like I blew a fuse or something. I haven't been with my family, all together in one place like that, since—I don't know, since I was little."

Anna closed her eyes and leaned her head back on the seat. There wasn't any radio in the car. It had been ripped out with all the other police equipment.

She said, "Sometimes I get this feeling—like a dream, only it's not a dream. Like I'm walking along, then all of a sudden I look down and I see that the ground's not right. It's not solid at all, I can see through where there are all these big yawning holes. And I think, *why is this happening, I'm just going along? I'm going somewhere!* But the ground's breaking up like clouds. I could just fall, and not end up anywhere. Did you ever feel like that?"

"If that happened to me," Dylan said, "I'd go like, *Hey, neat! I'm up in the clouds!* Like I'd figure, down there must be the place I'd already come from. Something like that. We should go up there together sometime, maybe."

Anna laughed. "Can I ask you something?" she said. "Did your parents really mean to name you backwards after Dylan Thomas? I mean, did they even know about him at all?"

"Oh, sure. My dad was from Wales, actually. He was like your typical cliché Welshman, used to crash around the house shouting poetry and singing when he got drunk. Well, I was a kid, I thought he made it all up himself. If you really want to know, my dad was a pretty half-assed poet. Half-assed drinker, too—one six-pack was all it took to do him."

"Took . . . to do what?"

"Killed him. He had a few beers with some buddies, then started spouting ol' Dylan Thomas, then . . . I guess there was some kind of a dare. Like he took a dare about climbing out the window of his buddy's car on I-84 and standing on the top. Reciting poetry . . . If he lasted long enough to recite any, I don't know. My mom is kind of tight-lipped about it. Anyway, she wasn't there."

"That is so sad. So sad . . ." Tears slid down Anna's face. She wiped them away with her skirt, but they kept coming. Her nose streamed and her jaw began to shudder. "I'm sorry—I'm sorry—I think I drank too much champagne."

Dylan stopped the car by the entrance to Anna's apartment complex. He pulled her over beside him on the seat and kept his arm around her while she snuffled and drooled.

"I'm all right now," she mumbled into his sweatshirt.

"You sure? You want to watch the alcohol, Anna. That's a hole you really can fall into."

"I don't even really like it."

"I could come in with you if you want, make you some tea, or a sandwich."

"No, that's O.K. But thanks a lot for asking."

JEALOUSY

Anna and Thorn sat in a booth at a coffee shop across the street from the main library downtown. Between them on the table were a folded page of onionskin bond, two small wrapped Christmas gifts, and two sandwiches. Anna's sandwich lay untasted on her plate. She'd only just pulled out the tiny plastic sword that skewered the layers together when Thorn told her the evil news. He was going away for Christmas.

"What about you?" he asked, beginning to eat. "Will you have a tree, a big family celebration?"

Anna grimaced. "No. My sisters won't even be home this year. Vonda's staying in New York, and Rennie has to go to Dave's family. Right after Christmas, my mother's going skiing with some pustulous bureaucrat from her office."

"Is that wise of your mother," Thorn said, "leaving you all alone?"

"What's she got to worry about? You'll be in Seattle."

Anna could see from his raised eyebrows that her attempt at flippancy had failed. He seemed genuinely offended by her mother's lack of concern. But even mothers deserved a break sometimes, and hers had no reason to fear. Anna wasn't about to do anything dangerous. She said it would only be three days. She'd probably hang out most of the time with Dylan.

"His girlfriend's going to California over break, so we'll be kind of in the same boat."

Thorn remarked that she'd been spending a lot of time with Dylan lately.

"Yeah, I really love him."

Anna watched Thorn dispatch the rest of his lunch, then push the plate away impatiently. His eyes were hooded; perhaps his thoughts had already returned to the manuscript on his desk in the library.

She said, "Sometimes I feel like that kind of love—that you have with your friends?—it's really the best kind. Like, even with your family, your parents . . . When you're little, they fill up the whole sky! But all the time you're growing up, it seems like they're shrinking. One day you could wake up and find they're too small for you."

She'd been fiddling with the plastic sword from her sandwich, twisting and bending it in her fingers. Now it sprang away onto the floor. She got up to retrieve it.

When she'd settled back into the booth, Thorn said pleasantly, "Are you going to sleep with him?"

"What?"

"With your little boyfriend." His smile thinned. "You said you loved him best."

"Not like that!" Anna laughed at the absurdity. "I never even thought about it. Really."

"Would you tell me if you did?"

"But . . . that's ridiculous! Dylan doesn't want me. He's madly in love with this girl Nicole."

Thorn's knife-gray eyes made tiny cuts in her assurance. She could feel it all leaking away. But of course he was just teasing, so she said, "Oh, I see you're jealous."

"No. Sometimes I even like to imagine you making love to someone else. I'd like to see you in all sorts of situations . . . to test your paleness against the darkness of the world. But this boy is too ordinary, too *mundane*," said Thorn, using Anna's own pet expression.

"You don't even know him!" she protested. "Why do you talk that way? That's like something my sister Vonda would say. She always tries to make everything out meaner or uglier than it is."

Thorn held up one finger close to her face. It was like a teacher's trick to catch her attention after her little outburst. When she was caught, he touched the finger to his lips, then to hers, where there was the tiny scar from her bicycle accident.

"In your life, everything should be lovely and rare," he said. "I think . . . I'd like to see you make love to a woman."

How did they get into this weird conversation? Thorn's concept of lesbian love seemed definitely a bit Victorian . . . like erotic postcards . . . Then something more serious, something about the way his voice had lingered on the words *lovely* and *rare*, started another thought.

Anna said, "Do you remember that time we were looking at those Chinese vases, and you said . . . You said how a person could go through a whole lifetime and just know two or three really perfect moments? I was thinking, about the first time, when you . . . when we were drinking tea, and you touched me . . ." She couldn't look at his face as she said this. "Do you think that was a perfect moment?"

Now, perversely, she thought, wasn't there a line of greeting cards with that name, *Perfect Moments*? Sentimental cards with pastel girls in sunbonnets?

"Every moment with you is perfect," said Thorn.

Anna frowned.

Thorn reached across the table to take her hand. "I'll tell your fortune, shall I?" He traced the lines of her palm with his fingertip. "Your nature is very fine. It craves everything to be like itself—lofty, serious, difficult to attain. Right now, you're feeling disappointed with me for speaking frivolously. Didn't you realize? I spoke cruelly to you on purpose, because you dared to love someone else, besides me."

Anna's hand jerked, but he closed his grip on it.

"Now open your present," he told her. He laid the little brightly wrapped package on her palm.

"It's beautiful wrapping." In spite of what he'd just said about her loftiness, Anna took refuge in this mundane observation. But it was very special paper: red, with a Chinese character handpainted on it in gold.

"Did you do this?" she asked. "What does it mean?"

"It means love," he said. "Elaine painted it. She wrapped the present. I love the way your eyelashes flutter down, like moths killed on a light. Are you weeping?"

Anna shook her head no.

"Don't weep," said Thorn. "Open the present. I chose it myself, only for you."

It was a book, an antique book with a soft Morocco-leather cover, the corners framed with tiny gold-tooled scrolls. Inside, the pages were blank; only one or two had lines of writing in faded brown ink. The paper was thick and creamy, heavily edged with gold. Anna closed the book and felt the gold edges seal together to form a cool metal band.

"This is beautiful," she said. "Thank you."

"For you to write your poems in," said Thorn. "Then will you still show them to me?"

"I don't know. It depends on if I mess up."

"You won't mess up. You write well, Anna." He touched the folded paper by his plate. "I only wish any of my students wrote half so well as this."

"But if I write on these pages they'll get wrinkly, then the edges won't be perfect anymore. I'll be intimidated to write."

"You shouldn't be." He took her hand, both hands, and held them between his own and brought them to his lips, the way a man might cup a flame and breathe on it to give it life. "You need to trust yourself more, Anna. And trust me, because—"

He paused. It seemed to Anna that the air inside the coffee shop, the atmosphere of the planet, the entire known and un-known universe swung and spun around that silence. It was a cosmic vortex; whole suns could drop into that void and disap-pear forever. He was going to say, *I love you.*

"Because I want you to," he said.

"All right." She stabbed the plastic sword into her bread.

"Now shall I open yours?" He picked up the other, even smaller package.

"No. You have to wait until Christmas."

She laughed at his disappointment as if she meant to tease, but in fact she felt suddenly, violently insecure about her gift. It was utterly useless and weird. It was a carved green button from the bin at the Veterans' Thrift. When she and Dylan had found it, her mind had somehow warped into thinking it was a charming caprice.

Thorn said it was time for him to get back to his desk. He folded her poem around the tiny present and tucked them into his pocket. They stood together for a minute in the rain outside the coffee shop. Thorn reached around and gave her shoulders a quick squeeze. She turned to press her wet face against his coat.

"Merry Christmas," he said.

The pedestrian light flashed *walk.* She watched him cross the street. She was holding her breath, holding in the scent of warm wool.

Three days after Christmas, the rain was still coming down. A forecaster on the six o'clock news said this could be the start of a twenty-year cycle: cloudy summers and winter rain, rain, rain. Anna went back to her room and wrapped the pink bedspread around her shoulders before she laid out her next game of tarot solitaire. If this was Las Vegas, she figured she'd have won $645 on the cards. If you didn't count the fact that she'd cheated.

What she wanted to do was call Dylan, but it was still too early. His mother wouldn't be out of the house for another forty-five minutes.

Dylan's mother was a nurse. Or not exactly a nurse, he said, but she worked in a nursing home. Her hours were really strange, and when she was home Dylan said don't call because she might be sleeping.

Anna's chest hurt from sitting hunched over the cards. And

her right thumb ached. She wondered if she could be getting carpal-tunnel syndrome. That seemed really depressing, to be barely sixteen and already have a syndrome. She decided to risk calling Dylan, but she would only let the phone ring one time, then hang up. Maybe Dylan would get the message and call back.

When she picked up the phone, there was no dial tone. Dylan's voice was already on it.

"Hey, Anna, is that you? Good timing!"

"I was just going to use the phone . . ."

"To call me?"

"Oh. No. Pauline." Though it seemed pointless to lie. She just felt embarrassed for some reason.

"Well, will I do? I'm bored out of my tiny brain here. I thought maybe we could go somewhere."

Anna agreed to meet him in half an hour—no, an hour. She wanted to wash her hair first. They could drive around and then maybe decide what to do. Dylan had half a tank of gas but zero cash. Anna had her mother's bank card. Maybe they could drive to an ATM.

While she was dressing, Anna thought how just for once she'd like to go out on an actual date. Hanging with Dylan didn't count. Thorn was the only boyfriend—if you could call him that—she'd ever had. But he was always so cautious about going places with her in public. Usually if they went anywhere they arrived separately and tried to behave like casual acquaintances.

Presumably Dylan went on dates with Nicole, if she was ever available and he ever had ten cents that didn't go straight into his gas tank. Dylan was a master strategist when it came to scrounging cheap meals, abandoned clothing, or free entertainment.

It was weird how Anna had never met Nicole, and Dylan had never met Thorn. As if their lovers existed in separate worlds or something. If you could believe Dylan, Nicole was utterly beautiful, fascinating, and good. Privately, Anna suspected she was a royal bitch. The way she strung Dylan along, made him wait and beg for every crumb of attention . . . Nicole used his feelings like a doormat while she stood on the threshold of her marvelous dancing career.

Anna also suspected they hadn't done much, sexually. Dylan seemed to shy away from that subject. Of course, Dylan was a lot younger than Thorn, less experienced. Though evidently he'd had other girlfriends before Nicole, some of whom might have been less elusive. Anna didn't need to be experienced herself to guess that Thorn was an unusually inventive lover. She should be grateful she hadn't had to learn like other girls, groping around with some spitty adolescent in the back seat of a car.

Anna still had Nicole on her mind an hour later as she perched with Dylan on the stone parapet of a roadside view point, high on the hillside overlooking the river. This rest stop had been officially closed by the police, on account of drug trafficking that used to go on there. Dylan had parked the car at Big Bob's Burgers at the bottom of the hill, and they'd hiked up in the dark, slithering and stumbling over wet roots and getting massacred by blackberries.

The view was worth the climb. A Christmas moon broke through the clouds. The river gleamed behind black screens of firs. An opal rainbow shimmered in the mist above Chinook Falls.

"Do you think it's dangerous to be here at night?" Anna asked.

"What are you afraid of, the highway patrol, or evil criminal drug dealers?"

"I guess the police is more likely, in Westview."

"That's why, you will observe, I didn't bring my banana boat up here. But tonight I feel like nothing can fuck me up. I can write the story of my life any way I choose." Dylan jumped up, raising his arms and pirouetting crazily at the edge of the parapet.

"Sit down, you idiot!"

Then, thinking of Nicole, Anna asked him, "Do you believe in happy endings?"

Dylan collapsed in a bony heap beside her. "If it's the end, you're bound to feel sad, don't you think? Unless you're just glad to be out of it, of course. Are we talking about anything specific?"

"Just life."

"Oh. Well, in that case, I want to be happy, sure. I want to start out happy, and push it as far as I can, why not? It just makes sense, nobody's looking to be miserable."

"You don't think, like, happiness is kind of a trap? You box yourself in, because you're afraid of not being happy, then you miss out on what's really . . . I mean, the way I feel about Thorn, it doesn't make me *happy*. But it's bigger than that. Like the moon on the river, or the wind moving the trees . . . They make me feel . . . not happy . . . *huge.*"

Dylan didn't answer. He was looking away from her, at the view. She looked down at his hand, beside hers on the balustrade. It was large and bony, like the rest of him. If there'd been more light she knew she'd see his hands weren't terribly clean, and the knuckles were roughened across the backs. The nails looked gleamy, by moonlight. She wanted to run her finger along them like piano keys, but couldn't think of any excuse to do it. He would think she was too weird.

"The way I see it," said Dylan finally, "like a story—here's a beautiful girl, crazy for some romantic dude . . . Or the other way around, some guy loves a girl. Why do you have to write the ending? There's enough in it already to get happy about, if you work it right. Well, isn't there?" Now he sounded almost angry. "What's Thorn's problem, anyway?"

Anna fired up, too. "What do you mean, his *problem*?"

"Why can't he be content with a good thing? Why can't you?"

"Thorn says contentment is for cows."

"Yeah, well. I never talked much to cows, but they seem O.K. with me."

Dylan stretched out along the parapet with his hands behind his head, staring at the moon. Then he did a kind of cat flip, twisting and landing on his feet. He seemed possessed with aimless energy and careened around the deserted rest stop, yelling kung fu and cartwheeling over picnic benches, walking on his hands, colliding with trash cans. He came back and flung himself against the balustrade beside Anna.

"O.K., this is what I think!" he declared.

She could feel the heat rising off him in waves.

"Whoa, breathe hard, why don't you?" She laughed. "Is this some epoch-making decision? You're about to alter the fate of mankind?"

"I'm working on it." Then he spoke quite softly, so Anna had to lean close to him to hear. "I think, you don't have to be anybody special, like a fucking poet, to feel miserable. But for contentment, you have to be a philosopher."

He leaned his head against hers, so the whisper buzzed across her cheek and made her shiver. "Or else a cow, maybe."

"That's fine for you to say!" She turned her face away. "What if the person you care about doesn't love you back, what then? How can you feel contented then?"

"Just let me be where I can hear her breathe," said Dylan.

They stayed silent awhile, watching the river. Anna discovered she was listening to herself breathe.

Dylan said, "Now I want to ask you the same question. Do you seriously think this guy Thorn loves you? Did he tell you so?"

Anna shrugged irritably. "What difference does that make?" This wasn't the same question she'd asked him, and the way he asked was aggressive, like he was trying to catch her out, or score against her somehow. "Anyway," she said, "half the time when people say *love*, like *I love* something, actually what they're talking about is food. Did you ever think about that?"

"Well, why not? I seriously love food!"

Anna threw up her hands in exasperation. But she recognized that Dylan had turned aside some confrontation that briefly loomed between them.

"In fact," he went on, "if I could have a choice right this minute between holding Nicole in my arms or a big, fat, juicy grilled hamburger loaded with onions, and the sauce oozing through the bun . . ." He sighed and laid his hands on his stomach. "That would be a tough call."

Dylan said you could get a pretty decent meal at Big Bob's

by clearing off the tables before the busboys got to them. As long as you did a neat job and left the tips alone, they mostly didn't harass you.

Anna was appalled. She knew Dylan was usually on the scrounge, but this seemed like something homeless people would do.

She said, didn't he go to school the week his health class talked about hepatitis? "Don't you ever eat at home?"

"There's never any food at my house. My mom kind of forgets about eating a lot of the time."

"Then what do you live on?"

"When I work, there's usually unclaimed pizza at the end of the shift. That's kind of my staple."

They started back down the hill to Big Bob's. In the dark Anna kept losing her footing. Dylan told her to walk right behind him with her hands on his shoulders. But he was too tall, even below her on the slope, so she held on to his waist. She could feel his muscles tense and relax as he walked.

Anna absolutely refused to cruise Big Bob's. They could get something to eat at her house. Her mother had completely stocked up before going on her ski trip. In Anna's mother's equation, guilt equaled groceries, especially, for some bizarre reason, frozen chops.

Once they were back in the car, on Riverview Parkway, the traffic slowed to a creep.

"This is insane," said Anna. "What's going on at ten o'clock on a Thursday night?"

"There must be an accident," said Dylan.

"No, it's a fire. Look, you can see the smoke!"

As they crawled around a bend in the road, a deep orange

glow appeared in the sky. *Like dawn in hell*, Dylan said. They both suddenly realized they'd been hearing sirens all the time they'd been up at the view point, but the view faced the wrong way for them to have seen the smoke and commotion.

The police were diverting traffic down B Street.

Dylan leaned out his window and called to the cop, "Hey, what is it?"

"Hurlbutt School. They're saying the boiler blew. Lost the whole building, looks like."

"Looks like is right! Thanks, officer." Dylan powered the window back up.

"I went to Horace S. Hurlbutt," said Anna, "for middle school. Everybody made jokes about horse farts, and the Horse's Butt school, but it was a neat old building. The varnish was so thick on some of the floors you could see into it, like amber. And there was this glass case in the vestibule with all of Horace Stanley Hurlbutt's medals from World War I."

They drove slowly around the park behind the old school. Then Dylan pulled off the road by the baseball diamond. It was starting to rain again. From inside the car they couldn't see the actual fire, but they could hear it, roaring like a distant war. Suddenly they heard a *boom* and sparks fountained into the sky.

Dylan said, "What do you bet that's the roof caving."

"This is so weird," said Anna. "You know, tonight? Before you came over, I did a tarot reading. And for the end card I got—this is really weird—I got the burning tower. Like it's got flames and sparks coming out the top, and a man and woman are falling screaming out the windows . . ." Anna got distracted wondering if they were the same man and woman as the lovers.

"Sounds intense," said Dylan. He stretched his arm along the seat back. "What does the card mean?"

"It's a scary one, like total disaster. Only I got it upside down. I think that's supposed to mean like freedom at the cost of ruining what you had before. And there's a bunch of other stuff, false accusations, false imprisonment . . . In this case, maybe it just meant literally a burning tower."

"That's pretty spot on."

He turned toward her slightly. She could see the orange sodium lights from the ball park glittering like sparks in his eyes. There was something strange about Dylan tonight. She'd noticed it ever since they'd been at the view point. Energy seemed to crackle off of him. Suddenly Anna realized he was going to kiss her.

She breathed faster. The muscles of her pelvis tensed. A year ago she might have passed the feeling off as social nervousness. A year ago she wouldn't have felt it at all. Now she knew it was sex. She was turning to butter just sitting there thinking about sex.

Behind the clamor of her own thoughts, Anna could hear Thorn's voice, like a voice loop repeating over and over, *Are you going to sleep with him? Would you tell me . . . ? Would you tell me . . . ?* As if because he'd said it, it was fated to happen.

Then what about Nicole? If Anna got off with Dylan, she could spoil things for him with Nicole. And it was Nicole he truly loved, you could hear it in the way he spoke of her, like spontaneous poetry. *I just want to hear her breathe.* Anna shivered and hugged her damp coat close. She wanted suddenly to weep and be comforted. To have someone adore her, the way Dylan adored Nicole.

Dylan's fingers brushed her coat sleeve. "You feeling O.K.?" he asked. His voice had a little burr in it.

Anna said wildly, "I got your hair in my eye!" She covered her face with her hands. "Christ, what'd you do, cut your hair with a weed whacker?"

Dylan said about twenty times he was sorry. He put his hands back on the wheel. Then he took them off and scrubbed them through his crazy haircut.

"I don't know. I mean . . . I cut it myself. A guy I was talking to, he said he had this foolproof system. Like for the perfect haircut? See what you do is . . . is, you take like a tuna-fish can or something. And you cut out the top and the bottom, so then you can pull your hair through, a little piece at a time, you know? So you can whack it all one even length. You don't even have to see it, right? It's foolproof. Only, I had kind of some trouble holding the hair and the can and the scissors . . ."

The moment had passed. Everything felt back to normal.

Anna said, "Let's go to my house and get something to eat. Then I'll cut your hair."

"You can cut hair?"

"I don't know, I never tried."

They drove home in comfortable silence. Anna told Dylan to pull into her mother's tenant-reserved parking space. She slid out of the car and was scrounging for her keys in her coat pocket.

Dylan came around the back of the car and gripped her arm, a silent warning. "Wait a minute, Anna," he said softly. "There's somebody by your door."

Dylan was right. A man stood in the shadow of the big rhododendron bush. Now he stepped forward. The door light gleamed on his hair.

"*Thorn,*" Anna cried.

"Anna. I was afraid I'd be skulking here all night."

"But why are you here? I didn't expect you back all week . . . And you never come here!"

Thorn shrugged lightly. He stood with his hands in his coat pockets, not trying to claim her or anything. He introduced himself to Dylan with easy politeness. "I hope I'm not interrupting anything," he said.

In reply Dylan stumbled over his own name, as if he'd never said it before.

Anna nudged him with her elbow. She didn't want Dylan to come across as a dufus to Thorn.

It seemed so bizarre to see them both together. Somehow Anna had got it in her mind they could never meet, as if they existed in parallel universes. Dylan was actually taller than Thorn. She wished she could crack him open and make him reveal his sweet nature, his energy, his poetry.

Perversely, now she even wanted Dylan to appear sexy. Not that anything could happen between them, but just because Thorn had despised him as a rival.

Dylan scratched his head, making his hair stand up worse than before. "Well, I guess I'll shove out," he said.

"Wait, aren't you coming in to eat?"

"No, I'll scrape something up at home. G'night. Nice to meet you, uh, Thorn."

As Dylan drove away, Thorn leaned Anna against her door and began to kiss her face.

"Is your mother coming home?" he asked.

"Not till tomorrow."

"I want to make love to you on your own bed. I want to see your books, and your dolls . . . Do you still have dolls?"

"Only one." Anna had trouble finding breath for words.

"She . . . was my grandmother's. She's celluloid. And her nose is . . . all dented in."

"Open the door, Anna."

When they had made love and Thorn lay stretched on her narrow bed, Anna got up to light a candle. She slipped her arms into a pale Chinese silk wrapper she had bought off a thrift stall at the market. The silk was rotting but it felt supple as water. This was the only time she'd worn it.

She crouched beside the bed.

"Did you utterly hate my button?" she asked. "I felt such a fool about it afterwards."

Thorn said he'd found it very intriguing. He'd been at Dex and Carlotta's on Vachon Island when he'd opened the tiny package, and they'd all tried to guess the symbolism of the carving, and the gift. Anna asked who was Carlotta, but Thorn ignored her question.

"He's very fascinated with you, my friend David Dexter. He always asks about you."

"Ugh. He's so . . . old."

"Youth is merciless." He smoothed her hair. She leaned her head back, so he cupped it in his hand. "I love how your throat pours into your breast. Dex is three years older than I. People tell me he's a mighty lover."

"He has a bald spot."

"Cruel girl. I brought another small present for you."

"Oh! What is it?"

It was a poem. Thorn had written it on plain paper, folded in three like a business letter. Anna's fingers trembled as she opened it. The poem was titled simply *To Anna*. It was about the fool on the tarot card.

In the poem, the fool stepped off the precipice. As he hurtled down, he spread out his arms with their fluttering sleeves. The arms changed bone by bone into wings.

"But at the end," Anna cried, "at the end, I don't know if he's going to fly, or smash himself to pieces on the ground!"

"No," said Thorn. "Neither do I."

EIGHT OF SWORDS

Anna propped the card against a book on her desk. The image was of a maiden standing bound and blindfolded. Swords made a close fence surrounding her. Anna leaned her chin on her hand and murmured, "What does she fear? What danger . . . ?"

Her mother tapped on the bedroom door. "Anna? Are you talking on the phone?"

"Not right now."

A whiff of perfume entered the room with Anna's mother. "What are you doing?"

"Working on something," Anna said.

Her mother spotted the tape recorder under some hastily spread-out homework papers on the desk.

"Oh, *that's* what you were talking to! I thought you were on the phone . . . Is this a school project? May I hear?"

"Not now," said Anna.

But her mother reached across her and pushed *play.*

The tape began where Anna had set it:

February 3rd. O.K., um, Tarot Poem . . . draft two. Trimeter lines, sort of uneven feet . . . um, Eight of Swords. O.K.

Eight swords thrust in the earth.
What danger, then? she thinks
twisting her hands uselessly
eyes restlessly moving
beneath the band. Rust
blooming along blades' edges
eight hilts stand up unclasped
by bound hands.

Anna hit *stop.*

"Don't listen to that!" Her voice was edged with irritation directed at herself, mainly, for letting the tape run on. Insecure people (*like me,* she thought) were always scheming to get surprised by praise.

"Oh, it's the *card,*" her mother exclaimed, picking it up to examine. "Ugh! This is gloomy. Why don't you choose one of the pretty ones?"

"Why are you being so damned perky?"

Her mother flushed. "Please don't talk to me like that!"

"Sorry. You just kind of broke my concentration, coming in right now." Anna moved things around on her desk, displaying restrained impatience for her mother to get to the point for this interruption.

"I didn't mean to say your poem wasn't good, Anna. Really. The image is just a little disturbing . . . don't you think?"

Anna sighed. "Was there something you wanted?"

"Well, I . . . I just wanted to touch base. I thought I might go out for half an hour, for a coffee."

"With . . . ?"

"Oh, just Walt from the office." Her mother laughed, perky again.

On an impulse Anna said, "Can I ask you something?"

Her mother had been tidying crumbs of dried fern from a defunct arrangement off the desk top, sweeping them over the edge into her hand. She looked up. "Now?"

"Are you in a big hurry?"

"No! Oh, no . . . What did you want to ask?"

"I was wondering . . ." Anna began. Meeting her mother's gently inquiring eyes, Anna felt her idea losing steam, going flat. A second ago it had seemed the answer to everything. "I wondered, could I go to New York next year? Like a junior year abroad, sort of. I could live with Vonda and go to a New York school."

"I couldn't let you do that!"

"Why not? I could even do correspondence courses. Vonda—"

Her mother interrupted. "Vonda has her own way to make in the world."

"So what? So do you. So does everyone."

"Don't sulk, Anna. Vonda couldn't take care of you, she's not your mother."

Anna's mother reached out to squeeze her shoulders, but Anna twisted in her chair. The hug fell short, just pawing her arm.

"It's not like you spend all your time around here baking cookies," Anna said. "Dylan drove me to the dentist, last time I had an appointment. I hardly even see you weekends, you always have to work."

"Of course I have to work, if you're planning to go to college. I'm still paying for Vonda's!"

Were those tears in her mother's eyes? No, it was just glare on her contact lenses from the overhead bulb. The harsh light brought out the tiny lines in her face, cast the saggy places into relief. She looked tired, and fragile.

"Sorry," Anna said. "I didn't mean anything."

"It's not as if you want my company even when I am around. You sit in here with the door closed . . ."

"Sorry." Again. "It's just . . . New York . . . I was talking to Ms. Swisser about some of the colleges there. They have extension programs for writers. Couldn't you just think about it? We could talk about it some time when you aren't busy."

"Ms. Swisser really thinks a lot of you. I ran into her walking her dog . . . You remember, last Tuesday, when it was so icy, and no school? *Trying* to walk her dog, I should say!" Anna's mother looked around vaguely for some place to sit, but there was only the unmade bed. "Well, Ms. Swisser went on and on about you. She said your writing has matured just incredibly this year. You know, Anna, you really have an excellent opportunity right here in Westview. Most high schools can't offer anything like Ms. Swisser's workshop classes."

Anna nodded absently. She pulled the tape recorder toward her. "I guess I better get back to work. Before I forget all my ideas."

"All right, then. I'll leave you to it."

Anna's mother put out her hand more slowly this time. Anna took it and rubbed her cheek on it.

"Night, night," said her mother.

"Listen," said Anna, "I think I'll go spend the night with Pauline later, O.K.?"

"Anna, it's late already."

"Pauline's got her license now. She can pick me up."

Her mother worried her lipstick with her teeth. "I'm not

really sure I like you spending so much time at Pauline's. Why can't she come over here? I don't even know her mother."

"Pauline's mother is an ultra-Christian," Anna said. "She wouldn't let Pauline come over here tonight because *you* won't be home."

Her mother's gaze fluttered away, to the bed again, to her own clasped hands. "But, Anna . . . Sometimes I can't help thinking, you girls seem so secretive. You never talk to me about what you do together."

Anna twitched her shoulders. "So what do you and Walt from the office do together?"

Anna's mother went out, closing the door gently behind her. After a few minutes Anna opened it again, a crack. She heard her mother's key rattle in the front-door lock.

Anna thought, why did people live in families, anyway? After they stopped being little children, she meant. People in families tore each other up. Like Anna, fawning on her mother's hand, then sticking her with a guilt trip. Twisting it in, like a knife. She hoped Walt would be nice to her mother tonight. As for herself, she'd really do better living with Vonda. Vonda never pretended to care about anyone but herself.

Anna punched on the recorder and rewound her unfinished poem. Then she erased it. Everything she tried to write these days was inane. She'd started to recycle garbage through Ms. Swisser's workshop—some of it stuff she'd written for assignments in eighth grade.

She ran the tape back some more, to another failed effort.

I walk, and walking call, and calling weep,
through cold and windless corridors of shell:
the chambered nautilus, each cell a door . . .

She could hear herself off-mike on the tape, muttering as she'd scribbed out lines.

> *each cell a door,*
> *where I must knock and pass. A passage*

No, the *passage. The* way.
The way is coiling inward to the heart . . . of the dark wood or something. Shit!

Anna shut off the machine.

She'd promised the nautilus poem to Thorn, but had never sent it. He had suggested she try reading her base material aloud, to get a sense of the flow and where the breaks ought to fall, before committing to a form and meter. Her problem was, she'd got stuck in the shell. She'd never figured out how to make the jump from that image to the goddess grove with its inward-winding path, which was what the poem was really supposed to be about.

She wished she could call him up and talk to him about it. Thorn usually went out with his friends on Friday nights. Even if he was home, if she called him, he'd be doing something else. She could always tell by the way his voice sounded, distracted, indulgent. The way people talk to children when they're too busy to listen.

The empty apartment seemed to echo around Anna. She thought she might as well go over to Pauline's, though she'd have to walk. Pauline had her license, but her mother rarely let her take the car. Between loving Jesus and lean-hipped strangers from country-music taverns, Pauline's mother had too much need of it herself.

Anna put her hands over her ears, pressing flat-fingered, then cupped, making patterns out of the silence in her room. Pauline was an exciting person to go places with. Left on their own, she and Anna quickly grew bored with each other. They couldn't even agree on a video. Pauline would want to raid her mother's liquor cabinet. Anna closed her eyes. She imagined chill, nacreous moonlight, a path winding between trees . . . Another fifteen minutes spent contemplating her pathetic attempts at poetry and she'd be ready to get falling-down, throwing-up, forgetting-everything drunk.

But then Dylan called. Anna talked with him for an hour and a half, before his mother came home and yelled at him to get off the phone.

Anna checked the locks on the doors, turned off the lights around the apartment, and went to bed. Her mother was still out, "having coffee."

DISGUISE

Anna unearthed the tape recorder from among some mounds of unsorted laundry her mother had been dumping at the foot of her bed. Weeks had passed since Anna had recorded anything on her diary, not since before spring break. Now she actually had something interesting to tell.

First she made the tape spool backwards a while. She punched *play*.

March 7th, her voice began.

> *Today I was listening to Mary Rose Cameron and one of her clones in the back of biology lab. They were having this huge discussion about people's sex lives . . . like, surprise! . . . Basically all that crowd ever talks about is sex, getting high, and how much they hate other people.*
>
> *They hate everybody. They hate each other, whichever one of them isn't in the conversation right at that moment. That's why I think Pauline seems to be getting kind of sick of them. Though Pauline's been cutting school a lot . . . Maybe that's just why I don't see her eating lunch.*

Anyway, I was going to tell about the conversation. It was graphic. They don't seem to care who hears every gory detail. Mary Rose is screeching, He had it up her ass, *and Mr. Gusterson comes up and says,* I told you to mark the frog's liver in purple. *And she's,* O.K., whatever, *and goes right on . . .*

The machine went silent, except for the whisper of cassette reels turning. When Anna's voice started again, it sounded different—slower and duller.

People like Mary Rose . . . like Pauline, even, they make me feel . . . I guess the word I want is probably inadequate. *Maybe I'm just jealous because it seems like they at least enjoy their lives.*

I really wonder . . . I wonder, is it so much fun for them, like they make it sound? Do they have orgasms? Do I? Sometimes my head's so full of what I'm thinking, and what's going on with Thorn and me, I wonder—how do you know if it's arousal, *or just mainly stress if you get excited?*

No, that's not true. When . . .

There was another long pause on the tape. Anna began to wonder if she'd maybe messed up the machine.

Then,

I feel like I'm made of mud *most of the time! But when I'm with Thorn, he touches me, and everywhere his hand touches I can feel the heat, and my life blooming inside. Sometimes I get this kind of sick shaky feeling like a junkie waiting for it to happen, it's not really pleasure, I—*

Anna hit *stop*. She said, "Oh, great, my life as mood foam."

Then she punched the buttons for *record*, not caring if she taped over the end of her last entry.

*May 9th. Guess what. Thorn invited me to a party! Some-
body he knows is having a party at a mansion up in Sunset
Heights. Thorn knows a lot of rich people, not that he cares
about it himself, but a lot of them are kind of patron-of-the-
arts types. Anyway, this is the coolest part, the party's a
masked ball. Everybody who's invited gets a robe, like a
monk's robe with a hood, and a carnival mask. So nobody at
the party's supposed to know who anybody else is. Thorn already gave me my robe, and one for Pauline, too.*

Thorn had said, "Here's one for your little friend, so you won't have to come alone."

Anna caught him up on it, saying, "Why do you call her lit-tle? Pauline's four inches taller than me, and two years older."

Thorn laughed and answered that Anna was deeper. How could he find out Pauline's true depths? It would be like trying to look into water with sunshine and reflections flashing off the surface.

Anna spoke to the tape:

*For some reason Dylan is acting incredibly pissy about this.
I mean, you'd think he'd understand how I feel, I hardly ever
get to go anywhere with Thorn. I told him,* It's not like I
don't want you or anything, *but he isn't invited. Thorn only
gave me just the two robes. But if Dylan won't drive us I don't
know what we're going to do, because there's no bus, and
Pauline's lost her driving privileges . . .*

Anna could guess the reason for Dylan's uncooperative mood. Things weren't going well with him and Nicole. He spoke about her less and less, and when he did he sometimes used an unfamiliar sarcastic tone. Once he'd said Nicole was "missing on one cylinder," and laughed obnoxiously.

So Anna tried to be patient with him, but this time he really had pushed her past the limit. He actually pretended to believe this party was dangerous, as if she'd need him for protection! He seemed to forget Thorn would be there.

"All these masks and shit," Dylan had said. "What is this, a cult? You have no idea what some guys will get up to if they think nobody sees—"

"Oh, like girls are any different," Anna'd cut in. "There's this huge myth that girls are so clean, they won't even scratch or pick their noses if nobody's watching."

"The guys I know'll do that if you're watching or not. I mean serious shit, here. I'm talking about you could get hurt."

Clearly his brains had warped from childhood exposure to midnight slasher movies. Anna reminded him that the people at the party did actually know each other.

"Nobody's going to be there who wasn't invited, duh. They couldn't get in without the robe."

"Yeah, well, you don't know them. And you won't know jack-shit if somebody drops a torpedo in your drink."

"O.K., so I won't drink!"

"You shouldn't anyway. But that's not the point, Anna. The point is, there's guys out there who'd rape their grandmothers if they thought they could get away with it. And for all you know, darling Thorn and his pedo-buddies—"

That's when Anna totally lost it and started yelling. *"What's the matter with you? Where is this coming from?"*

Dylan backpedaled then, saying he just thought Thorn asked too much of her sometimes. "I feel concerned about you, is that O.K.?"

"No, it's *not* O.K. Because Thorn always will ask too much, he'll always go too far. He won't settle for what's ordinary. Thorn told me once, if he can't be good, at least he'll never be petty."

"Oh, swell," said Dylan in his new sarcastic voice, "so if he can't be an ordinary decent guy, he can at least be a total asshole. Is that it? Is that what you admire?"

Keeping a grip on her temper, Anna had said, "You always oversimplify things. Everybody isn't just straightforward, white or black, true or false—"

"Well I am," he'd said, "and I'm telling you the truth. You can call me petty if you want."

Anna stared at the numbers mounting on the tape counter. The tape kept winding while she recorded nothing. She sighed and switched off the machine.

She should've told Dylan that she didn't think he was petty. That he was sweet to feel concerned. Sadness had made her insensitive and mean.

She felt sad all the time these days, all the time she wasn't with Thorn, and sometimes even when she was, because she'd be looking at him and thinking, *he will leave.* Already this was May, his sabbatical year was nearly over. Even if he decided to spend the whole summer out West, he'd have to be back in New York before the start of classes in September.

Sometimes, too, a sense of the approaching end affected Thorn, making him cruel and demanding of her. It was as if he had to twist the last drop of delight out of her, before she slipped from his fingers.

So this was part of the reason she couldn't listen to Dylan, with his dire predictions that "something would happen." The future rushed toward her like a blank wall. *Something had to happen!* Otherwise, everything would just . . . crash.

The evening of the party was unseasonably warm. The sun shone still, though shadows had fallen over Sunset Heights. The blue of the sky and the green of the hills appeared electrified by a dark underpainting of storm clouds.

Dylan drove. Pauline sat beside him in the front seat. She'd pushed back the hood of her robe, revealing bright new hair like dandelion fluff on the thin stalk of her neck.

Anna had got in the back seat so she could change into her robe. She hadn't wanted her mother to see her leaving the house wearing it. She'd said she was going to spend the night at Pauline's.

Pauline said, "You're not going to wear your clothes underneath that, are you?"

Anna had planned to do just that, but as soon as she pulled the heavy black cotton robe over her head she realized she wouldn't be able to bear the heat. She began to squirm out of her jeans, using the robe for a tent.

"Don't peek," said Pauline to Dylan. She ran her fingers over his cheek and down the tight cords of his neck. Pauline would flirt with a fire hydrant, if nothing better came down the street.

Well, good luck to her, trying to strike a spark off Dylan tonight. He was still fuming over this party. He hadn't spoken two sentences to Anna since he'd picked her up at the bus stop in front of Thriftway.

Anna stripped off her shirt; then, in a spirit of defiance, her bra and underpants. She dropped them on top of her heap of clothes, which she pushed onto the front seat, beside Pauline. Pauline flashed her a thumbs-up.

Dylan stared straight ahead. The westering sun shone through his ears like stained glass.

Anna sat quietly thinking how she would spend the evening with Thorn, walking around among other people, but with the robes of secrecy cast over them . . . like the cloak of invisibility . . . two naked and anonymous lovers, risking everything and nothing to be together.

In a way she imagined it would be like that night long ago after the reception for Rosemarie Barkis, when wine and sleep together had transported her onto an astral plane. That night Thorn had seemed to her like a god, a tremendous force of nature blowing through her body, her soul, her mind. Nothing had been left apart, divided and doubting, nothing alone and fearful.

Dylan broke through her dream. He said, "What's with you, Anna? You haven't let out a word, hardly, since you got in the car."

"She's dreaming up all the evil fun she can have when no one will know it's her," said Pauline. "It's these quiet, deep ones you have to watch out for. When they decide to cut loose, whoo-ee!" She laughed and waved Anna's bra out the window at a passing convertible.

Dylan steered the big Ford up the switchbacking streets of Sunset Heights. The higher they rose, the grander and more secluded the houses became. Anna glimpsed blossoms foaming over garden walls, or the flash of white pillars behind wrought-iron gates. Palaces of cedarwood and glass thrust like isolated rock formations out of the cliffside. Below, the flat land east of the river still basked in sunshine. Beneath the shadowing hills, lights spangled the city.

A red paper Japanese lantern hung above a gateway in a stuccoed wall.

"Stop here," Anna called to Dylan.

A silent figure in a monk's robe waited to let in only those who wore the required disguise. Anna and Pauline snapped on eye masks and drew up their hoods as they slid out of the car.

Dylan leaned his head out the driver's window. "What do you want me to do?" he asked. "If I can find a place to park, I can wait around for a while. Or I could come back—"

"Thanks, but we'll get a ride down with Thorn," said Anna. "I don't want you to waste your evening. You've been sweet."

She bent down and kissed him. His lips parted in surprise beneath hers.

The kiss stayed with her as she walked up the graveled drive with Pauline. Anna laughed and said she'd always wanted to do that. The laughter was to counteract a slight aftertaste of guilt. She'd been totally jerking him around tonight.

Pauline answered that she was surprised Anna hadn't gone after Dylan before. Because Dylan was hot, obviously, and it didn't look like that Nicole had been keeping up with the demand.

All around them in the overgrown garden, colored lanterns glowed. They caught sight of robed and cowled figures flitting among the shadows, and heard low laughter and an occasional shriek, like birds in a tropical forest.

When they came to the house at last, it looked nothing like the trim and chem-lawned developers' mansions that had sprung up all over the hills around Westview. It was old, built in a Spanish style with cream-colored stucco and a red-tiled roof. An un-Spanish climate had swollen the surrounding garden, so now monstrous shrubberies pressed against the windows and slimed the red tiles with wet, spent petals. Mosses splashed over the terrace. A greenish bloom crept up the walls.

On a broad paved terrace in front of the house, the party was already in full swing. Music played and people danced. The sounds of laughter and clinking glasses floated down to the garden.

As Anna and Pauline came up the steps, they saw several people waving their arms, signaling and making bizarre gestures.

"What the hell are they doing?" said Pauline.

"I think they don't want to talk, so people won't recognize them from their voices," Anna said. Which made sense. But, she thought, it also made them look quite mad.

A burly figure detached itself from the crowd and rushed, arms outstretched, to greet Anna and Pauline. Unlike the others, this man wore a full face mask, a leering devil with its tongue thrust out and gilded eyeballs. Anna thought it looked Chinese.

The devil engulfed Pauline in a hug and swung her up the remaining steps to the terrace.

"Someone fetch this delicious girl a drink!" he roared.

Partly to escape the same treatment, Anna stuck out her hand and started to introduce herself. She guessed this must be the owner of the house, a Mr. Nordholm, Thorn had said. He cut her off with a hand pressed hard over her mouth.

"No names," he cried. "No names!"

The tobacco taste of Mr. Nordholm's fingers lingered unpleasantly on Anna's lips. She loitered by the top of the steps, trying to make out which of these whirling, gesticulating figures might be Pauline. Soon a slim person took Anna's hands and drew her, too, into the dance.

Anna felt a rush of excitement. Usually at parties she stayed glued to the wall. Sometimes she talked with other girls, whose eyes were rolling around in search of somebody more interesting.

Now she couldn't even tell if her partner was a man or a woman. A woman, she thought, but without hearing the voice it was hard to be sure. People switched partners randomly. As soon as one partner turned away, Anna lost her—or him—into the free-for-all. But a new turn brought someone new to dance or talk with.

It was fun to try to make out people's conversations if they were using sign language, or to make up new gestures for more complicated ideas. Of course, plenty of people were talking, and no one was going to recognize Anna's voice, anyway.

Pauline reappeared briefly by Anna's side to say she was going into the house to look at something with Gunnar.

Who was Gunnar? And how did Pauline meet someone so quickly? During the whole evening Anna saw Pauline only twice again. Once in the house, she recognized her by her laugh. And once in the garden she saw a person she thought must be Pauline cavorting in a stone-rimmed fishpond, her robe hauled up to reveal bony white legs and the curve of a pink-flushed ass.

The noise level rose on the terrace as heat and alcohol loosened people's tongues. Anna helped herself to a handful of strawberries from a cut-glass bowl and went down into the garden to look for Thorn. By now she knew he wasn't on the terrace. She would recognize him, in spite of any mask.

In the garden Anna joined a game of blindman's buff. The "blindman" had pulled his robe around back-to-front so the cowl covered his face. At first the other players fled shrieking in every direction. But when someone called *freeze* they had to stay in one spot. They crouched or twisted or bent away from the blindman's groping hands.

This seemed like more fun than Anna usually saw adults having. Though she had no way of knowing how old any of these people might be. Sometimes a thing like a hand or the curve of a middle-aged stomach under a robe gave her a clue. She wondered if they were all free spirits like Pauline, or if they mostly lived conventional, dull lives. Perhaps they dreamed of excesses committed in disguise.

While she was zoning, the blindman blundered near. Anna held her breath and stood perfectly still so he wouldn't sense her presence, but with a sudden wide sweep of his arms he caught her. He ran his hands over her face, touching the tiny scar over her lip. He touched her breasts.

Anna flinched, but his grip on her was strong. He pulled his cowl down and began to kiss her, crushing her mouth, thrusting his tongue. He was Thorn.

Anna closed her eyes and surrendered to the kiss. The moment seemed electrified by the current of fear she'd felt before. Now, just as in her fantasy, they were making love in full view of everybody. Thorn slipped his hands up the loose sleeves of her robe.

A man came over to them carrying two green-glass goblets filled with white wine. He handed one to Anna and one to

Thorn, then clinked each glass with his heavy gold ring, like a toast.

Later, Anna lost Thorn again. They had been dancing on the terrace, and Anna went into the house to get a drink of water. She found the house rather confusing. Many of the rooms were dark, and many doors were closed. Opening one in search of the kitchen, Anna came upon a scene out of some Roman orgy, with flickering candelabra and naked limbs entwined in snaky knots. The walls and floor of the room were splashed with—

She certainly hoped and believed that was red wine and nothing worse. Anna closed the door sharply and went back out to the terrace. She felt like Bluebeard's wife.

Now she couldn't find Thorn. Maybe he had gone inside looking for her. No way was she going to open any more doors. A passing figure handed Anna a green goblet. She carried it with her into the garden.

The moon was a silvery smudge in a swollen purple sky. Anna found a stone bench by a bank of flowering shrubs. The air smelled rich with impending rain and obscure vegetable sexuality. She sipped her drink. There was nothing wrong with it, of course. Date-rape drugs had been part of Dylan's lurid scenario. Though she would rather have had something with ice.

She rubbed at a line of sweat under her breasts. She wished she hadn't been in such a hurry earlier to make an ass of herself, and had kept on her bra. She pushed back her hood and undid the top buttons of her robe.

Hands gripped her shoulders from behind. The wineglass sloshed onto the grass.

"Oh, you frightened me," Anna cried, half laughing, half angry. She was getting a little weary of sudden shocks.

The man standing behind her massaged her shoulders lightly through her robe. His hands moved forward. She could feel the rise and fall of his breathing against her back. She saw a gold ring on his finger.

Anna jerked her shoulders. "Please don't do that!"

He didn't answer. His fingers slipped under her collar, then played up and down her throat. They began to press lightly on her windpipe.

Anna drove her heels into the ground and rocketed up from her seat. The man clutched at the open edges of her robe. She screamed and twisted against his hands, tried to lash out at him with her feet. The bench was in her way. She staggered against it as he dragged her toward him.

Then he let go. Anna fell and struck her knee on the bench. When she looked up, she saw they were no longer alone. Another man had come upon them silently and hooked his arm around her attacker's neck. He hauled him backwards, up on tiptoes, then punched his head once. The blow made an appalling woodchop sound.

Anna's attacker sagged, gurgling and flapping his hands. The other man let him drop. "Let's get the fuck out of here," he said in a low voice.

They ran across the dark lawn. They were running in the wrong direction. Grabbing his hand, Anna started to zigzag back, toward the house and the lighted terrace. She stumbled on her trailing robe. He caught her before she fell.

He held her, and she leaned into him, pressing her face against his chest.

"Thorn," she said, breathing him in, breathing in warmth and comfort and a tang of . . . gasoline.

She looked down and saw six inches of ragged pants cuffs sticking out below the hem of his robe.

"What the hell are you doing here?" she spoke between her teeth. "How did you get in?"

"Over the wall," said Dylan in his normal voice. "It took me hours to find you, too."

At first, he said, he'd lurked in the dark corners of the garden, afraid of being noticed and expelled. In one out-of-the-way spot he'd witnessed a man strike a girl and knock her down.

"He just hauled back and let her have it, *pow*! If this is the kind of fun you like, Anna, I don't know, but—"

"But how did you get the robe?" Anna interrupted him.

"I persuaded fists-of-steel to loan me his."

"What, he just handed it to you?"

"After I fed him a few knuckles, sure."

Anna pulled away from him. "Are you telling me you hit somebody else, too? What is it with you and the gestapo tactics tonight?"

She began fussing with her costume. It was a mess, all twisted up. The fabric stuck to her knee where she'd banged it on the bench. She only now realized how much it hurt, and the pain made her unreasonable with Dylan.

He said, "Who are you calling gestapo? I just rescued your ass from that rapist, in case you failed to notice."

"Oh, he was not! He was just some garden-variety scuzz-bucket who got carried away with this anonymous business."

"That's not how it looked to me. I warned you something like this could happen." He made his hand into a fist and stood clenching it, watching the torn knuckles jump. He said, "I don't mind telling you now, I'll be good and relieved when Mr. Wonderful Thorn goes back to New York, where he belongs."

"But I'm going with him," said Anna.

"What!"

"I said, I'm going to New York." She had to stop to clear her throat, it felt so dry. "I'm going to live with my sister Vonda."

Dylan was just standing there waggling his head. Like he was some stupid toy with its head on a spring.

At last he said, "You can't stand Vonda."

"She's my sister, isn't she? It's not like I haven't lived with her before, and survived."

"Have you talked to your mother about this? Have you talked to Thorn, even?" His voice rose. In another minute he'd be shouting at her. "Anna, I'm not trying to piss on your parade, but from a guy's perspective Thorn's had a pretty fucking brilliant setup here! All his rich ass-licking friends—and girls—and anything goes because he can just cut all the strings and take off at the end of the year—"

She shouted back, "I won't listen to you! That's a disgusting, dirty-minded, cynical way of looking at things." She turned and began to walk, limping a bit but quickly, back toward the house.

"Anna—" He trailed after her, pleading now. "Anna, just tell me, was this his idea? What did he say about this?"

She didn't answer. How could she, since she hadn't mentioned anything to Thorn about her plan? But she would, and he would be glad. Glad! She was only waiting till she could work her mother around to it, then she would.

Anna stopped. Dylan bumped into her. She stood watching a group of men coming down from the terrace and around the side of the house, toward them. A couple carried flashlights.

One heavyset man wore a mask pushed back on his forehead. She thought it must be the devil mask.

She said, "Dylan, you need to leave here right now."

He took hold of her sleeve. "Come with me, then."

"No! I'm really grateful to you, honestly, Dylan. But just go away *now*, before you get in trouble. That man coming over here is Mr. Nordholm. He owns this house."

"Fuck him," said Dylan.

He just stood there, waiting. The men, four of them, including Mr. Nordholm, surrounded Dylan. One of them said to Anna, "You're O.K. now, honey. He won't bother you anymore."

She tried to tell him Dylan wasn't doing anything, he was her friend. But everybody started shouting at once. The whole bunch of them were circling and shouting, making terrible ugly noises, like a dogfight. One guy kept sticking his flashlight in Dylan's face. He grabbed at the front of Dylan's robe, yelling, *He's the one, he's the one.*

The man wore a terry-cloth dressing gown instead of the monk's costume. He said Dylan stole his robe and tried to beat up some woman. Blood started trickling out of his nose as he yelled.

"Bullshit!" Dylan roared. "You hit her yourself, asshole!"

He broke free from their hands and took a swing at the bloody nose. Anna didn't see him connect, but the man fell. She heard other blows strike home, and men's wordless voices panting, or grunting, or sucking vainly for air. Then somebody smashed a flashlight down on Dylan's head. He staggered. Mr. Nordholm stepped in and caught him in an armlock.

The man in the dressing gown sat on the ground, clutching

his face. The gown gaped open, revealing plump white thighs streaked with dark blood. The other men frog-marched Dylan down the gravel drive to the front gate. Anna trailed after them, crying at them to please, *please* listen a minute!

By the gate she saw Thorn. She ran to him, and he caught her by the shoulders. He tore her mask off, not seeming to notice that it pulled her hair. He held her jaw and turned her face from side to side under the light by the gate, searching it—for tears? bruises? His lips were drawn in a hard line.

"Gunnar told me there'd been trouble," he said. "I've been searching for you—but you're all right? Nobody hurt you?" He passed his hands once more, lightly, over her face.

"No, but, Thorn—it's Dylan. He came looking for me and now I don't know what'll happen—"

She saw lights flashing beyond the wall, out in the street. Somebody yelled, *Police!* A knot of people crowded around the gate.

"Oh my god, they're going to arrest him!" Anna broke away from Thorn. She tried to claw her way through the people blocking the gateway. "Let me *out.*"

Thorn pulled her back. In her craziness, she even struggled against him.

"Anna, no! Listen to me! You're underage. You've been drinking. That's right, calm down. Now look at yourself." He touched her where the robe sagged open. "If the police get one glimpse of you, we'll all spend a night in jail. Some of us may be lucky if it's only one night."

She couldn't meet his eyes. The way he'd said—*you've been drinking*—was it so obvious? Was everything that had happened because she couldn't control herself?

Thorn set two fingers under her chin and raised her tear-streaked face. He smoothed her hair back and straightened her robe. A couple of buttons were missing, but he fastened the top one so the gap wasn't obvious.

"I'll talk to Gunnar Nordholm," he said. "For his own sake, he'll want to lay this mess to rest as quietly as possible. We'll go back in and put on some clothes now. Then in half an hour I'll drive you down to the police station and we'll pick your friend up. How does that sound?" He tweaked the end of her nose gently.

Anna said in a small voice that her clothes had been left in Dylan's car. She didn't know where they were.

"Elaine will have something you can wear. She's been staying at the house with Gunnar."

By now the crowd around the gate had broken up enough so they could see out to the street. Thorn made Anna stand well back, and away from the light. There were at least two police cars out there, still with their flashers going. Anna could see Gunnar Nordholm standing talking with one policeman and another man she didn't recognize from the party. The policeman scratched up the back of his head and stared at the notebook in his hand. His shoulders hunched aggressively. Anna guessed he was weirded out by all these men in black robes. She saw no sign of Dylan.

The man she hadn't recognized came back to the gate. Anna saw that he'd removed his mask and unbuttoned the front of his robe. Underneath he wore a uniform and a badge from some security company.

Thorn hailed him. "Can you tell us what's happening with the boy?"

"They're taking him in." The man used a broad palm to plane sweat off his forehead. "Silly fool put up a fight, he was trying to climb right back over the wall when the officers arrived at the scene. You ask me, he's lucky nobody didn't blow a hole through him, crazy bastard. Pardon my French, miss."

"But he's just a boy!" said Thorn.

"Yeah? They're the ones you got to watch out for, nowadays."

DISCOVERY

Hours passed before Anna got to see Dylan again. First Thorn took her into the house, where he made her drink coffee and wash her face. In an upstairs bedroom she changed into loose gray sweats which made her look like a cow but would hopefully conceal her lack of underwear.

She went down to the kitchen to find Thorn already changed, wearing an ink-blue linen jacket and tan pants. He'd polished his hair back so you wouldn't notice it was long. He looked elegant and old.

"My respectable disguise," he said to her.

Thorn introduced her to Gunnar Nordholm. The big hearty voice that Anna remembered from behind the devil mask matched Mr. Nordholm's broad weatherbeaten face, but not his eyes, like tiny chips of ice. Shrubby little white-blond curls grew down in a peak on his forehead. He looked at least forty-five, maybe more like fifty. Thorn said Gunnar collected Chinese jade and antique wooden sailing boats. Anna wondered what he had shown to Pauline.

"Pauline!" she cried. "Where's Pauline? I haven't seen her, and she needs us for a ride home."

"She's gone," Thorn said. "It seemed wiser, since the police have already been here once tonight. Dex drove her."

"Dex . . . ? He was here?"

"You didn't meet up with him? He'll be disappointed. Look," he said, drawing her to a window. "The rain's started. I expect the party will wind down pretty soon now, anyway."

People were coming in from the garden, blinking at the house lights. Many had already stripped off their masks. They stood around in little groups, chatting and laughing over-brightly, like parents at a school event.

Thorn drove Anna down to the Sunset/Westview police station in his little old convertible car, with the top up. She waited while he went in to see if they were finished with Dylan. But he came out again almost immediately, and alone.

She clutched his sleeve before he was even fully in the car. "Wouldn't they let you see him? Is he hurt? Does he need a lawyer?"

"Gunnar withdrew the complaint, Anna. They've got nothing to charge him with. But they don't handle juveniles here, evidently."

After questioning Dylan, the police had sent him on to the county Juvenile Reception Center over in River City. They'd only hold him there until they could get in touch with his parents, Thorn said, so Anna really had no need to worry.

"His mother," Anna said. "His father's dead. But she works nights and a lot of weekends. What if she isn't home?"

Thorn sighed. "Do you want us to go over to River City and find out?"

"Yes, please."

He started the car, then sat for a moment staring out the windshield at the spattering rain. Anna noticed a star-shaped crease mark where she'd clung to his linen sleeve. The long pale bones of his hand tensed over the stick-shift knob.

Thorn put the car in gear and pulled out of the police-station lot. He took a right turn for the River City bridge.

He said, "All right. But for god's sake, Anna, be careful how you behave, what you say in front of any juvenile welfare people. We're walking into the lion's den, there."

Anna sat knotting her fingers in her lap. "This is all my fault," she said.

"Don't blame yourself. That rent-a-cop Gunnar hired to watch the gate was overzealous. He called in the heat without consulting. Gunnar was furious—but not with you."

Soothing words. Still, Anna had never felt so miserably aware of the difference in age that divided them. She had gone as his guest to a sophisticated adult party, drunk two glasses of wine—not even that, since she'd spilled most of the second one—and wound up messy and in tears, causing trouble for everyone, needing to be picked up and dressed and her knee bandaged like a kindergartener.

By now it was past midnight. They found the parking lot for the complex of county correctional offices mostly deserted. Blue signs, like highway department signs, directed visitors to the court, judges' offices, Adult and Family Services, and Juvenile Reception, all housed in identical low brown boxes linked by islands of institutional landscaping. Anna spotted a police cruiser parked near the entrance to Juvenile Reception.

The cop was just coming out of the building as Anna and Thorn approached. Anna recognized him at once. Plump brown mustache, brown springy hair—he rubbed his hand up the back of his head as if to tip an imaginary hat as he passed by. She'd last seen him talking with Gunnar Nordholm.

"Excuse me, officer," said Thorn, stopping him. "We're looking for a boy? He got picked up earlier this evening for causing some disturbance at a party. Westview said he'd be here."

The cop seemed to draw himself in, to become suddenly squint-eyed and lean. "He might be."

Thorn said, "Perhaps you could tell me—"

The cop cut him off. "Mind telling *me* what happened to that boy's face?"

"His face?" asked Thorn. "Did something happen to it?"

"Oh, you didn't see that part, huh? Want to tell me just exactly what you were doing at that party, sir? And who is this young lady?"

Thorn answered with weary politeness. "We seem to be talking at cross-purposes, officer. My name is Arneson. I'm a teacher. As for what the boy or anybody else was doing at the party, I have no idea, as I was not invited. My young friend here telephoned me at home because she'd heard he was in trouble. You know how it is with kids, they're on the phone half the night. I offered to look into the matter in case the boy's mother was unavailable."

The cop snorted. "Oh, she's *available.* She'll need a ride if she expects to take her son home tonight."

Thorn said he'd brought a car. He pointed it out, parked behind the cruiser.

The cop, momentarily distracted, said, "That a 2000? Haven't seen one of those in a long time."

Thorn smiled. "1600," he said. "There's room in the back for a third passenger, if he's got limber knees. I don't know about four. Perhaps if the ladies can double up . . ."

The cop snorted again, this time with laughter. "I take it you never met the *lady,* huh?" He seemed to be relaxing. His stomach expanded over his belt again. But suddenly his attention swiveled to Anna. "You at that party, miss?"

"Me? Oh . . . no."

"Are you sure? Because if you were, we'd certainly like to have a word with you about it."

"I wasn't there." Anna felt the lie rise to her cheeks and crawl up under her hair.

The cop stood looking at Anna and stroking his mustache down over his lip. "Don't like to see juveniles at an adult party," he explained to Thorn. "Especially not this one."

Then he squatted down in front of Anna as if she were a little kid. He put his hands on her shoulders. "Let me ask you something else, miss, if you don't mind. This fellow your boyfriend?"

Panic stopped her breath before she realized he must mean Dylan, not Thorn.

"Just a, uh, *friend* friend." She bent her head so her hair fell forward, over her face.

"Well, let me give you a piece of advice, from an old-timer, all right?" He winked at Thorn. To Anna he said, "You look like a nice young lady. A good student, too, am I right? So take a tip from Officer Gerrard: You can do better for yourself. Choose better friends. End of lecture. All right?"

"All right." Ridiculously, Anna wanted to cry.

The cop stood up and gave her shoulders a little friendly shake before letting her go. Then he said to Thorn, "It's not my business to be giving out information, sir, but I will tell you this. Tonight's not the first time we've seen this particular young man. He's the type, always running in the street. Don't they give out homework at school anymore?"

"I certainly do," said Thorn.

The cop nodded approval. "Well, I'm not talking major offenses with this youth. Just the usual punk stuff—truancy, defacing public property, creating a nuisance. But that kind of attitude can be the tip of an iceberg. 'Nother couple months, and he'll start to be charged as an adult."

What was he saying, Dylan was doomed to a life of crime because he'd cut classes and skateboarded in the Thriftway parking lot? Anna's shoulders jerked restlessly. Thorn flicked her a tiny warning frown.

Thank god, the radio on the cop's belt began to sputter, and he walked away from them to take the call. He raised his free hand in a goodbye salute. "Good night to you, Mr. Arnold!"

"Thank you, officer," said Thorn.

Thorn said to Anna, "The mother's already here, I think, from what the officer said. Do you still want to go in?" He paused for her to answer, or look up. "Do you need to take a minute for a few calming breaths?"

Anna nodded gratefully. Thorn leaned against the edge of a battered picnic table, which along with a Japanese maple and some azalea plants formed a small oasis just outside the doors of the reception center.

"That's something I always notice in the Northwest," he said. "There's no public building, no matter how mean or utilitarian, that doesn't have its bit of gardening. In New York, the smell of officialdom is floor wax and disinfectant. Here, it's bark dust."

"I'm ready to go in now," Anna said. When Thorn pushed open the door to the Juvenile Reception Center, the first thing

Anna noticed was the smell—not bark dust—like a dentist's office. The room smelled like mouthwash.

The second thing she noticed—behind a counter protected by a glass partition was an office. And inside the office was another room. It was like a box with wire-reinforced observation windows. Inside, the box was empty, except for some metal benches like shelves, or doctors' examining tables, screwed to the walls. It looked like where they'd put you so they could watch you if you were violent, or crazy on drugs. Dylan was not there.

Thorn went over to the counter and tapped at the glass partition, but the woman seated behind it signed to him to wait. She was on the phone.

A minute later she slid back her window and said, "Please take a seat. I'll be right with you." She was a pleasant-looking middle-aged person in a flowered dress. She wore no badge or name tag to say what her job was, though it seemed very late at night for her to be all alone here, if she was just a receptionist. A counselor, maybe.

Thorn settled into one of the half dozen or so metal chairs lined up against the walls of the small waiting area. He reached his arm across the back of the seat beside him, meaning Anna should come sit there. But Anna felt too restless to sit. She prowled the area, reading posters. *Job Corps. Adolescent Anger Management Workshop. Child Abuse Awareness. End Handgun Violence!* A massive Pepsi vending machine hummed in one corner. From some unseen corridor came occasional echoing reports of heavy doors closing. Thorn shut his eyes and stretched his legs across the stained beige carpet.

At last the woman behind the counter called him over. Thorn

went through his *My name is Arneson, I'm a teacher* routine again, then asked about Dylan.

Anna came to stand beside him at the counter.

"There's no one here by that name," said the woman.

Thorn continued to smile pleasantly as he told her they'd just spoken to the officer who'd brought Dylan in. Of course he was there.

Anna said, "Dylan's his last name. His name is Thomas. We just came to make sure he's all right . . . if he needs a ride home . . . ?"

"Are you family members?" asked the woman.

"Sunset/Westview police informed me that the boy would be brought here," said Thorn. "If he is not being charged with a crime and is no longer formally in custody, we would like to speak with him, please."

The woman returned Thorn's smile. Then she said she was very sorry, but since they were not family members she would not be at liberty to disclose to them any information concerning anyone who might or might not be on the premises, or in the custody of the county. Toward the end of her speech she raised her voice slightly and cast significant glances at a huge surveillance camera mounted on the wall behind the glass partition.

Thorn turned to Anna. Before he could speak, she said, "We'll wait here till he comes out."

"Anna, perhaps we should go out to the car to discuss this?" He nodded toward the front door.

Just then, it opened. A man stuck his head in and yelled, "Dial-a-Cab!" He pushed his way into the room. "Cab call? Anybody here name of Dillon?"

Anna said quickly, "What name did you say?"

The cab driver fished in his jacket pocket for his dispatch sheet. "Got it here . . . Charlene Dillon?" He spelled the name out laboriously, "D-I-L-L-O-N. Called at 1:35 a.m., cab for . . . looks like, Mondago Avenue. From County Juvenile Office. You her?"

"See, he is here!" Anna cried, ignoring the question. "They just spelled his name wrong. It's D-y-l-a-n. Thomas Dylan." She turned to the woman at the counter.

"Not on his driver's license," said the woman. Then she pinched up her lips, because probably she'd violated some official rule by saying what she did.

But what did she mean? A buzzer sounded on the woman's desk. She held up her hand for Anna to be quiet while she picked up her phone and punched some buttons.

She parked the mouthpiece under her jaw long enough to tell Anna, "If you'd care to take a seat in the waiting area, I believe our crisis coordinator will be out in a moment, with Jeff and his mother." To the cab driver she called, "They're coming now."

Thorn was making signs to Anna like, *Calm down and come talk with me privately.* But frustration made her reckless and rude.

"Not *Jeff*," she told the counselor woman. "We're looking for *Thomas.* THOMAS." Like the woman was deaf, or stupid.

"Thomas Jefferson Dillon," said the woman. "Please take a seat. Mr. Blucher will want to speak with you, I'm sure."

The driver said he was going out to his cab. "You tell Miz Dillon, I'll wait fifteen minutes, tops, and the meter's on. That's company policy."

Anna found herself turning round and round, staring at the

woman, the doors, Thorn. Maybe only her brains were revolving. All that sad, beautiful story Dylan had strung her—the wild Welshman reciting Dylan Thomas as the wind blew him to oblivion—lies. All lies.

An unseen door banged. Anna heard voices and footsteps approaching. A uniformed policeman opened a door at the end of the counter. Close behind him came a woman, tall and hulking, clutching her purse to her stomach with both hands. She moved like a ship, all forward motion. A chair toppled in her wake. The cop squeezed himself back against the counter.

The counselor woman called, "Your cab's waiting, Mrs. Dillon."

Mrs. Dillon wheeled and bellowed, "Jeff! Where'd he get to?" She carried the mass of her weight high, in her bosom and shoulders, so she seemed on the verge of toppling over, to crush the luckless bystander with her rage. She wore dirty pink stretch pants and white nurse's shoes. A fistful of dubiously blond curls was knotted on top of her head with a lacy scarf. It quivered when she raised her voice. *"Jeffie!"*

Dylan came out with a second policeman following, still holding his arm. After them an older man in a sports coat, with his hands full of papers, stepped through and closed the door behind him.

A vivid bruise marked Dylan's cheekbone. His upper lip puffed grotesquely. His hair stood up in spikes, as if he'd run water over it, but dark patches of blood remained. Under fluorescent lights, surrounded by bulky men with guns, Dylan looked strange—distorted and shrunken and bleached. And his name was Thomas Jefferson.

He saw Anna. He tried out a smile that looked more like a

sneer, with his fat lip. "I can go now, I guess," he said. His voice came out slurred.

Mrs. Dillon said, "Just one goddamned minute, buster! You're not going anywhere till I say I'm ready. So squeeze it in your hand if you got to."

"Yeah, I hear you," Dylan muttered. "Anna, just come outside with me a minute. We'll be right by the door, Mom!"

Anna glanced back at Thorn. He nodded and spoke to the woman at the counter.

"I'll take the young people outside, if you don't mind."

The man in the sports coat spoke to Thorn. "Are you people friends of Jeff's? My name's Don Blucher, I'm a juvenile crisis coordinator." He came forward with his hand outstretched. His pale-lashed eyes flickered back and forth between Anna and Thorn. "If you'd like to step back to my office—"

Mrs. Dillon interrupted him. "If *you'd* like to get the cork out and hand over those goddamned papers, mister—there's a cab out there waiting, and if I got to pay extra while you sit here diddling yourself, I'm going to send the goddamned bill to the county!"

Mr. Blucher said, "We could all save some time, Mrs. Dillon, if you'd adopt a more constructive attitude . . ."

Thorn said to no one in particular, "We'll just go wait out by the picnic table, shall we?" His words were almost lost in the lava flow of Mrs. Dillon's wrath. He opened the front door and jerked his head for Dylan to exit.

Anna slipped out behind them.

The rain blotched Dylan's T-shirt. A rusty stain trickled over his brow. He stood by the picnic table with his arms crossed, glaring at Thorn. The attitude brought out a phantom resemblance to his mother. Anna thought, no wonder he'd never wanted her to phone his house while that woman was home.

Dylan said, "I didn't tell them anything, if that's what you want to know."

"I guess that's very wise," said Thorn.

"I guess that's very convenient for you. It wasn't my little crimes they cared about, those cops. They knew damn well you fuckers were up to something sick at that party."

Thorn said, "Anna, if you don't mind, I'll wait for you in the car. I think you need to have a private conversation with your friend."

He slipped off his jacket and draped it over her shoulders before he walked away. The warm smell of him in the cloth gave her some comfort.

There followed a moment of strained silence.

Then Dylan said, "Anyway, thanks for coming here."

"It's Thorn you should thank, really," Anna told him. "He talked Mr. Nordholm out of pressing charges, and went to the police station, and drove me around everywhere. I bet he would've even got you a lawyer, if you'd needed one."

"Yeah. Well." He started to rub the rain off his face, then stopped and felt over his bruised mouth with his fingertips. "Well, please convey my profoundest gratitude to that monkey's dick."

She said, "I don't think you have anything to say to me that I need to hear."

"Yes I do. I do!" He was breathing fast and unevenly. He took a step toward her, his fists knotted. He looked like he might kill her. She backed away.

"Anna! That ugly scene tonight—don't you understand? He set you up for that."

"What happened to me at the party had nothing to do with Thorn. And it was just some jerk, not a rapist, anyway."

He shouted, "How can you be so dumb? Where was he all that time? How do you fucking know it wasn't Thorn that did it?"

"I know!"

"Yeah? Well, what difference does it make if it wasn't him? If he just pimped you out to somebody else?"

Anna couldn't speak. She beat her hands against the edge of the picnic table—*no, no, no.*

"Anna—?"

"*No!*" She stared at him. She got this odd illusion that it was her own face that she saw, with the crumpled mouth and eyelids puffy from unshed tears. Her voice scraped in her throat. "Who do you think you are?"

"I'm your friend, remember? Someone who cares for you?"

"I don't even know who you are, *Jeff.*"

She left him standing in the rain and went back to Thorn's car. In the car, she began to shiver uncontrollably. Thorn started the engine and let it idle.

"The heat'll come up in a few minutes," he said. He chafed her hands and breathed warm breath on them. "Do you want to tell me what happened?"

"I never saw him like that before," Anna said, "so angry— and violent. It's like I never even knew him!"

"He's had a very difficult evening, I imagine."

"He lied to me! About his name, and I don't know what else." She squeezed her eyes shut against a vision of the battered face, stupid with disbelief, as she'd walked away. "Do you think his mother's really crazy?"

"Oh, no. Just very drunk. She could barely stay on her feet."

"He told me she was a nurse!"

At least, he'd said his mother worked in a nursing home. Maybe that wasn't a lie; maybe she did the laundry there, or emptied bedpans.

Thorn said, "The boy must've been pretty hopped up himself, tonight. He was certainly behaving that way."

"No, that's impossible. Dylan hates alcohol—and drugs—all that sort of stuff. He's a total prude about it."

"Is that what he told you?"

Anna fell silent.

"Poor Anna," Thorn said. "I'm so sorry about this evening. Maybe we can still make it better."

"That's O.K." She leaned her forehead against the cool window glass. She wanted nothing but to creep into her own bed and cry for a while in the dark, with the pink coverlet pulled up over her head.

She said, "Do you think you could give me a ride home now? I'm very tired."

"I thought you were supposed to spend the night with Pauline?"

"I'd wake her mother up if I went there now. I can just go home. My mother won't care."

"I want you to spend the night with me," Thorn said. "I want to watch you open your eyes in the morning. I think you'll look very sweet."

Anna swallowed painfully. She was getting a sore throat, maybe. "It's so late," she said.

"Then I won't have to wait very long for my pleasure, will I?"

Anna tried to make her stiff lips stretch to a smile. She felt too exhausted to argue about anything more.

THE DEVIL

Anna's mother tapped on her bedroom door.

"Anna? Are you in there? Open the door, it's locked."

"I can't . . . I'm doing something."

"What have you been doing in there all day?"

"Nothing."

"I can't hear you! The phone's for you. Are you going to plug it in there?"

Anna wiped her face on a damp fold of the bedspread. She couldn't raise her voice, it was clogged with slime and tears.

"Who is it?" she said.

"What? I said, some boy called Jeff is on the phone! Are you going to get this or not?"

"I can't . . . I'm busy."

"Anna?" Her mother's face appeared around the edge of the door. "Are you still up? That boy Jeff is on the phone *again*. Why can't you ever pick it up in here?"

"I don't know anybody named Jeff."

"Anna, he's been calling you constantly for weeks!"

"I can't help what he does."

Anna's mother came into the room and stood looking down at the cards patterned across the bedspread.

She said, "For heavens' sakes, how many fortunes can one person have? If you don't come out of your room more, nothing will ever happen to you!"

"I'm not telling fortunes," Anna said. "It's just solitaire."

Thorn lit candles and set them on the floor beside the futon. It was time for Anna to go home. She got up to look for her clothes. He sat at his desk chair watching her.

"Have you stopped eating?" he asked. "See how this tiny sharp bone casts a shadow. And this one." He touched her collarbone, her wrist, as she stood before him. His hand modeled the point of her hip. He sighed, a soft animal sound of pleasure.

How she loved Thorn's sigh. When they made love, she listened for that sweet release of breath. She'd come to think of it as the most perfect, sometimes the only truly safe moment of their time together. It was only then she could be sure he was satisfied with her.

Thorn said, "You've stopped sending me poems, too. Why is that?" His fingers dug into her haunch.

"I have to go home," she said.

"Are you writing the poems in the book I gave you?"

She hung her head.

"Anna, what has happened to your discipline? You disappoint me!"

She pressed her fingers to her eyelids, under her curtain of hair. Sticky tears leaked around them.

"I can't," she cried. "I can't write anymore!"

He chose to be gentle with her. He told her what she felt as a block was really a gateway. She mustn't panic, thinking there was no way through. Every level of mastery had its locked gates. She would not break through without leaving some blood on the splintered doors.

"When you first make love," he said, "you think you'll be content to flirt and fiddle forever. But the act is never consummated until you break the hymen. Then you learn pain, and the sweetness of new desires."

Just so she must rush the gates of poetry, he said.

"But what if I'm not ready?" Anna cried.

"Then it will hurt more, just at first."

She didn't even know what they were talking about anymore. She turned to pick her shirt up off the floor and blundered against a candle. It toppled, spilling hot wax on her foot. She sucked in a little cry.

She bent to right the candle, to touch the round red spots swelling on her bare foot.

"Are you hurt?" he asked, concerned.

Anna let out her breath. "No."

But she let him look at her foot and put some dabs of unguent on the marks. Anything so he wouldn't look in her face.

She couldn't tell him that she didn't believe it was a gate that stood in her way, but a hole. A vast, crumbling gap that used to be filled by the person she'd thought was Dylan. How could she rush ahead—how could she set her foot anywhere, when great holes kept opening up all around?

In the car on the way home Anna said to Thorn, "You scare

me when you talk like you did, about breaking things inside of people. What if the thing you break is the last strand? What if there's something else you didn't know about, ripping away at the other side? A person could shatter apart."

He answered, "Risk is an essential element of love, Anna. Also of poetry."

Anna felt thankful for the dark inside the car. Thorn wouldn't think she was so pale and fine if he could see her now, in a good light, with her damp nose and eyes red from secret rubbing.

She kept her eyes fixed on the white lines stretching away into darkness in the center of the road. Once, as the silence widened between them, she asked him, what was he thinking?

Thorn laughed. "I'm thinking of terrifying ways to crash your gates," he said. "But not just yet. This time, I'll send a poem to you."

A few days after school ended in June, Anna spent another evening at Mr. Nordholm's house. This time she went with David Dexter Fromm. Thorn had persuaded her to do it.

"Dex is enchanted with you," he said. "And, perhaps, I owe him a favor."

She'd come to Thorn's apartment in the afternoon to celebrate her last final exam. Now they were getting ready to go out for a stroll around his neighborhood, and maybe a coffee, before he drove her home to Westview.

She paused with one foot raised, her sandal ready in her hand. "This is a joke, right?"

"Let's call it a test."

She made a slight, foolish noise, not quite a laugh. "I thought I'd finished all my exams."

He spoke lightly, watching her. "Dex is, after a fashion, my boss, you know. My publisher. His desires matter to me."

Anna knew he couldn't really mean that, not the way it sounded. The teasing edge in his voice gave her the clue. She dropped the sandal and went to kneel by his chair. She traced tiny designs on his knee with her fingertips.

"I don't love Dex," she said. "Dex . . . what does he have to do with us?"

"What does anything have to do with us?" The edge in his voice was harder, cutting. "*Us* is a closed room. Like Rapunzel's tower—I creep in at the window, but there's no door, nowhere to go from here."

She whispered, "I don't know what you mean."

"Don't you? I'm not a little boy, Anna. I can't grow childish again, to come play in your room. You have to open the door, step out into my wider world."

Anna felt the blood drain from her heart. He was tired of her—was that what he meant to say? He found her childish, not sophisticated enough? Did he want to give her to Dex, to get rid of her?

"Look at me, Anna," said Thorn. "Don't look away."

She stared at him till his face began to shine like a bright undecipherable spot before her eyes, and all around was dark.

He said, "Let me tell you something, it's the secret of undying love. Too much sweetness blunts desire. Even for you, my very sweet Anna." His swift glance caught her flinching.

In her head the words began to pound, *The end. This is the end of everything.*

"I want you to go with Dex," Thorn said. "Can you, because I ask?"

She cried *no, no, no*. Dex gave her the heaves, she said. Why must he ask this of her? Why was it so important?

"Dex is not important," Thorn said. Dex was merely a door that she could open, or close in his face. "Is that the way you want our love to end," he asked, "because you lack the courage to go on? You have no curiosity to enter my complicated life . . . or don't you trust me, absolutely?"

Anna thought, it was true, what Thorn said. Pain and sacrifice made the bond between them closer than pleasure . . . There was not really that much pleasure. Thorn had warned her before, he always spoke the truth. It was pure, hard truth that made him seem cruel.

Still, her imagination failed, or her courage. Not her love. "How could I be with Dex, and then with you?" she cried. "Would you even want me any more?"

"More than ever," he answered.

"And it would be just the one time, just a little time, and that would be the end? I don't have to do anything more?" Anna clutched his hand to her lips. She tried not to gush and blubber like a baby.

Thorn disengaged his hand and passed it very lightly over her diaphragm. "Like the belly of a guitar," he murmured. "I can feel your music vibrating inside. Beautiful . . . We're not talking about the end, but about a new beginning. Both of us together, not you locked up in a child's life, and me alone outside."

Her eyes seemed filled with smoke, she could hardly see his face. But the future . . . For the first time in months the future was no longer closed and blank. She'd speak to Thorn about New York. After this little thing with Dex, she'd tell him about her plan . . . Anna felt the warmth of his hand against her breast and leaned into it gratefully.

Dex took her out to dinner first, just the two of them at La Farfalla. He didn't seem at all self-conscious about being seen with her in public. He respected her space, and behaved like a friendly uncle.

Anna actually thought it was funny, in a sort of diseased way, how she went through her life yearning for things, which finally arrived warped beyond recognition. This was her first date.

At the restaurant Dex told amusing stories and laughed just as hard when the joke was on himself. Anna watched with fascination the red lips opening . . . white teeth . . . red, pointed tongue. His laughter spilled out over the black beard.

Dex encouraged her to talk, too—about herself, her family, her hopes and dreams. She found herself telling him, not her "hopes and dreams," but an actual dream she'd often had.

The story of it wasn't always quite the same, but it kept the same elements. She'd be running across open ground, with somebody after her, shooting at her. Usually the setup was a prison escape, or from a Nazi concentration camp. Once she'd dreamed about running away from a gang of terrorists who'd highjacked her school bus. In the dream she could never run properly. She could barely crawl, her legs dragged uselessly. She would cower with her eyes shut, pretending to be already dead. She always knew they would shoot her anyway. And they did. She'd feel the bullets thudding into her body, and her legs would kick convulsively. Because it was a dream, the bullets didn't really hurt, of course. The horror lay in knowing they were coming.

Halfway through telling all this, Anna stopped. "I don't know why I'm thinking about this, now." She laughed inanely.

Though she did know, at least in part. It had something to do with the heavy gold ring on Dex's finger. She had to put her hand over her mouth to keep the laughter from boiling over and scalding everyone in the restaurant.

Dex drove Anna up to Gunnar Nordholm's house, where he said he often stayed when he came to town. All these rich people seemed to hang together. Dex was rich.

"He's not a clown, you know," Thorn had told her. "Dex is independently wealthy, which means he can finance a number of his own projects."

That made Dex an important man in the world of small-press publishing. Thorn's world.

Once at the house Dex's manner changed from jocular to insistent. They both knew, of course, what they had come there to do, so he had no need to play at romance. Dex was not a gentle man.

He had a compact muscular body. Anna tried not to look at all the hair. It sprouted even on his back. A black mat spread across his thighs and up the center line of his belly, where Thorn was smooth and defined.

Late that night Anna taped a segment on her diary. She said she'd felt like vomiting when Dex touched her.

She went into the bathroom and spent a long time staring into the sink. Then into the mirror above the sink. She touched her cheeks, rubbed raw by Dex's beard. A small bruise showed on her neck. But what she'd said on the tape was a lie. She didn't actually feel anything at all.

Anna stood in the hallway outside Thorn's apartment door feeling suddenly, desperately afraid to knock.

But Thorn expected her. He opened the door and drew her into his arms. He smelled so good, clean and familiar, like fresh sheets on her bed when she'd been feverish.

He said, "I feel your heart racing."

"I just ran up the stairs."

"Come in. I'll make some tea."

He brought a tray from the kitchen. They sat together on the futon, Anna cross-legged, sipping her tea, Thorn lounging against the pillows.

"How was it?" he asked.

"How was what?"

"Don't tease. You know I want to hear about your evening with Dex."

The tea she had swallowed wouldn't go down. It stayed in her chest, a hot lump. He ran his fingers up and down her spine until she shuddered.

"Tell me."

"It was . . . O.K. I didn't think about it too much."

He laughed as if she'd said something provocative.

"Poor Dex! He'd be devastated to hear you. He was counting on ravishing you away from me with his delightful antics."

Anna said, "I don't think he cared very much what I felt."

"Now you interest me extremely." Thorn sat up and moved around to face her. "So David Dexter is an insensitive lover!

But what do you mean, exactly? Was he stupid? Too quick? Did he hurt you?"

Anna looked away.

Thorn said, "Ah!" softly, as if he also felt pain. Or something else. "But tell me, did he take you someplace first? Did you have a pleasant conversation? Yes, I expected that. Dex would want to be the gentleman. Then he seemed a different man, in the dark? Or did he leave on the lights?"

Anna was starting to breathe fast. Her hands were too sweaty to hold the teacup. She set it carefully on the tray between them. She watched him with quick, furtive glances as he asked his questions. He always met her eye. He was smiling, loving her. She was his prey.

"Stop it!" she cried. "I don't—I can't remember all those things."

"Don't lie to me, Anna." He didn't smile anymore. He took her reluctant hands, rubbing his fingers over her palms, feeling the panic sweat. "Lies could destroy everything we have between us."

"But it's the truth! I tried not to think—not to be there. I closed the door. I don't remember what's inside."

"Then we'll have to break it open, and look."

"No."

She tried to pull her hands away, but he held on. They struggled briefly. Then they were making love. The tea things crashed to the floor. She had never felt so terribly excited. She clutched him with slippery fingers and screamed, as if he tore her.

They lay together, exhausted.

Thorn murmured through her damp hair, "You always evade me."

"It's not true! I did what you asked."

"Then you were too lovely and distracted me, when I wanted you to tell."

But she knew that sooner or later he would make her tell him everything. This was what it meant to love Thorn. He would never be satisfied by what she freely gave. He would seek for yet one more layer of reticence in her that he could rip away. So she was always freshly exposed and raw. She was always new for him.

KNIGHT OF CUPS REVERSED

Anna's mother said, "Don't you have anything better to do than play cards? It's a beautiful day! The whole summer lies ahead of you. Where are all your friends?"

"Pauline's at somebody else's. I called."

"What happened to the boy with the jalopy? Dylan. I haven't seen Dylan for a long time."

Anna laid out a new line of cards. The ace of swords was in the first place. That gave her a space for the king.

Her mother said, "I thought he was cute, that Dylan. A bit *grungy* for my taste . . ." She giggled like some stereotypical schoolgirl. "But if that's the *in* thing nowadays . . ."

"Mother, grunge is so not the *in thing*." Anna rolled her eyes, rolled her whole head, which always worked perfectly to kill conversational initiatives when Pauline did it to her. But her mother seemed impervious.

"You know," she said, "for a while I was wondering if things might be getting a little serious between you two. I was seeing so much of him, and he does seem like such a nice—"

Anna said, "He's got a rap sheet as long as your arm, if you want to know."

"Oh! Oh, Anna. Oh, I'm sorry."

"Why should you be? You didn't arrest him."

Anna's mother sat down on the bed. The cards slid all over.

She said, "Why do you take that tone with me? I'm only trying to understand you. To understand what's going on in your
life."

"Nothing's going on."

"How can you tell me that, Anna? Look at you, you've lost
weight—your eyes are like holes! I hear you crying in here."

She sat twisting her fingers together as if she meant to pull
them off. Anna might have felt sorry for her, but it was too
much . . . too much, to carry the weight of her mother's feelings, besides her own.

"Anna, tell me the truth, *please.* You're not taking drugs?
Or—oh, god—not pregnant?"

Anna even managed a smile at that. "No."

"Then what? A relationship? That boy Dylan? Or Jeff, who
keeps calling and you'll never talk to him? Please don't just
shake your head like that, Anna. I have a right to know!"

Anna's mother wiped away tears with her fingers, messily.
Anna wished very much she'd go away now, she didn't want to
see this.

Her mother said, "God! It's so unfair. Your first romance . . .
It shouldn't be like this."

"Look," Anna told her, "maybe I'm not totally joyous in my
life right now. O.K., I admit that. It doesn't have anything to do
with you. This is not a mother/daughter occasion, O.K.?"

They both sat looking down at their hands for a moment,
like a moment of silence for somebody dead.

Then Anna's mother began again. She kept eating her lipstick off as she spoke, so it took her a long time to get her sen-

tences out. She said there was something else she had to discuss with Anna. Something about Walt.

"Walt Durban?" said Anna. "The guy in your office?"

"Well, yes, Walter Durban. The guy in my life. He's asked me to marry him." Anna's mother unleashed the hideous girlish giggle again. It startled Anna into looking up.

That was a speck of blood on her mother's lip, not lipstick.

"And I told him," her mother said, "I told him . . . well, I said . . . no." But not no, *permanently.* Only, she felt they ought to wait, not rush into things. Heaven knew, she'd learned her lesson about rushing into romance. Besides, she had her family's feelings to consider, as well as her own. "But oh, Anna, I can't tell you how wonderful it is to feel cherished again, and . . . and attractive. I know that must sound terrible to you—two old people!" Her laugh rose and faded. "It's been so long," she said.

Anna knew she should make the effort to sound interested in all this. She said, "Why don't you marry him, then?"

Her mother had begun torturing her fingers again. She said she'd agreed they might possibly try living together.

"Just as a trial. And that brings me to you, Anna, because this is your home, too, and I'm not very happy about the kind of example this might be for you . . . And of course I could hardly not realize you don't feel very . . . well, *enthusiastic* about Walter. It's natural, you're young and he's not romantic-looking. So I've been thinking, and something that's occurred to me is what we've discussed a few times before, though I admit I didn't feel very comfortable with the idea . . . I mean about you going to stay for a while with Vonda, in New York. What's the matter? Isn't that what you want now?"

"Yes . . ." A blank mist floated before Anna's eyes. "*Yes*. It's just . . . such an incredible surprise."

Her mother said she didn't mean for Anna to go away permanently, of course. But she did think Anna could enroll in a Catholic school, that might be better than the public, in New York City.

"For one semester, anyway. That's what I told Vonda. Because I can see, Anna, that for whatever reason you're not very happy at home now, so it might really not be such a bad idea for you to get away for a little . . . But I told Walt we won't make any decisions right away. You can take plenty of time to think about it."

They sat together for a while longer in Anna's room. Finally Anna said she'd like to phone a few friends, tell them the big news. Her mother nodded but didn't get up to go yet.

Anna remembered to say congratulations about Walt Durban. She said he seemed O.K. to her, really. The words sounded so stiff and meager, she stood up and kissed her mother on the head, where the curls sprang back from her brow. Anna was surprised at how little and soft her mother felt.

At last Anna's mother went away, saying they could all discuss this more tonight, at dinner. Anna sat at the edge of her bed, breathing shallowly and fast. She was gripped by an almost unbearable agitation, as if her whole body had gone to sleep, and now to move any muscle, even to let the breath lift her rib cage, would expose her to the stabs of ten thousand needles. She supposed this was joy that she felt, but until the first grip relaxed, it hurt almost as much as despair.

Eventually she hauled out her phone and punched Thorn's

number. His voice when he answered sounded so far away. She couldn't picture what he'd been doing. Working, perhaps, not thinking about her.

Anna hung up softly. She wouldn't speak to him on the phone. She had to see his face when she told him about her going to New York.

Excitement was rising in her, forcing out numbness. She should get dressed. She could make the three-fifteen bus. Now she knew he was home, she could go there and surprise him. She'd never done that before. She felt she had to hurry, hurry, before her news exploded inside her like a bomb.

The downstairs door in Thorn's building was unlocked. Usually during the day someone would prop it open with a newspaper or something. In spite of the street life, cafés and bookstores and people panhandling on nearby Bellona Avenue, this wasn't a high-crime neighborhood.

Anna slipped up the stairs and tapped at his door. She stood twisting her fingers together until she realized how she must look like her mother. She tapped again.

Thorn opened the door. He wasn't wearing any shirt. But Anna didn't need that, she could see in his face, in the unfocused brilliance of his eyes, what he'd been doing.

Thorn let out his breath in a *whoosh*. He said, "Anna."

Then he stepped back from the door and said, "Come in."

She followed him automatically.

Pauline lay stretched with her long bare legs among the pillows of the futon. She sat up when Anna came in and stared around her wildly, as if someone had just stolen her clothes.

Thorn said, "Can I get you something, Anna? A cup of jasmine tea? Some wine?" He was smiling at her.

Anna stared back. Darkness rose up behind her eyes and made a tunnel, with his face, still smiling, far away at the bright end.

From some other planet Pauline's voice said, "I'd like a cup of tea." She seemed to have found Thorn's shirt.

"All right," said Thorn. He went into the kitchen. Anna heard him putting the kettle on.

She said to Pauline, "How long have you been sleeping with Thorn? All along?"

"No, don't worry, it's nothing like that," said Pauline. "You had him first, I swear. This is just, you know, like kind of a mess-up."

"Why should I worry?" Anna said. "He's not my possession." She couldn't believe how her voice came out, so light and smooth, with no trace of the darkness that was turning her blood to ice.

"God, I can't believe you're being so cool about this," said Pauline.

Anna laughed out loud. The sound brought Thorn hurrying back from the kitchen.

"I'm leaving now," Anna told him, still with that brittle lightness in her voice.

"No, Anna—wait!" A line appeared between his brows. He kneaded it with his fingers. His hand slipped down his face; he pulled distractedly at his lips.

He said, "I'll walk downstairs with you, all right?"

He drew her out into the hall and closed the door, not glancing back at Pauline. He kissed her there. He held her face in his hands and searched it, as if he feared it might show cracks.

"You're trembling," he said. "Why are you so lovely when you're sad? It unnerves me."

"I can't help being sad."

"You are so pale. You told me once you had vampire skin." He touched her like a blind man, his hands fumbling over her eyes, along her mouth and throat. "I'm the vampire, Anna. People like me—writers, poets—we suck up the juices of the living. I know you suffer . . . But I can't stop myself. I have to dig my fingers through all your emotions, to gobble them up. You knew this about me. I never hid from you, Anna."

"You hid Pauline."

Thorn made an irritable gesture, brushing flies away. "Pauline doesn't matter. I only wanted her because of you."

"Me!"

"Come," he said. "Come back inside with us."

He pulled her toward him. She kept her body stiff. She was afraid to bend, to move. A brittle sheen lay over the surface of her world. One step and she'd break through and drown in icy darkness.

She started to shake. His face appeared to glaze. In some crazy way she thought it was the ice that was covering her eyes.

"Don't make me," she whispered. "Don't."

"I understand." He sighed, and released her. "You're not ready, now."

"I'm not ready," she repeated.

"I'll walk you downstairs. Call me when you get home, Anna. Please, promise."

"All right."

He walked with her all the way to the bus stop, though he wore no shirt or shoes. Just before she got on the bus, he remembered to ask her, "Why did you come to see me today? Is there something wrong? Was it something important?"

"No," she answered. "Nothing important."

THE TOWER

When Anna got home she found the apartment empty. This surprised her. She thought her mother'd said something about dinner, but she hadn't been listening and couldn't remember. Maybe just that there was a chop melting in the bottom of the fridge for her.

She went into her room and pulled out the tape recorder. The diary cassette was in it. But the tape was almost used up, she'd have to start a new one soon. She snapped the cassette out of the machine.

The new tape, what would it have on it? Sex with Pauline? And what else? She began absentmindedly to pick at the tape where it was exposed, between the cassette reels.

Anna felt a stab of regret for Pauline. She'd always thought of her as a free person. A powerful person, not just a toy to get picked up and used . . . perhaps loaned to a friend . . . then tossed aside. She teased up a loop of tape with her finger. It unspooled smoothly from the reel.

Here on this tape were all the moments of her love for Thorn. She thought of them like a necklace of bright beads—perfect moments strung on a dark strand.

She remembered she had promised to call him when she got home. She tossed the cassette onto the bed and picked up her phone.

By mistake she punched Dylan's number instead of Thorn's. She didn't realize what she'd done until she heard the woman's voice.

"Yeah, who is it?"

Anna panicked and would have hung up, but Dylan's mother yelled at her, *"What the hell do you want?"*

Anna answered without thinking, "Dylan. *Jeff.* Is he there?"

"No, he ain't here. Who's this calling?"

"Can you tell me when you expect him back? This is Anna Pavelka."

"Oh . . . Well, tell you the truth, honey, I don't exactly what you'd call *expect* him. He's kind of living with friends right now, you know . . . Tell you the truth . . ."

The woman was mumbling, or not talking close enough to the phone. Anna thought she said he was sleeping at Nicole's.

Anna said, "Could you give me the number? Nicole's number?"

Mrs. Dillon burst out laughing. "That'll be the day!" Then she muttered something indistinct, like, *Mr. hotshot cell phone.*

"Please, Mrs. Dillon, I really need to speak with him."

"What'd you say your name is?"

"Anna. I don't know if you remember, but I was at the Juvenile Reception Center that night Jeff got arrested at the party?"

"You from the county?" Mrs. Dillon's voice grew loud. Her breathing rasped in the phone. "Because if you are, I told you people already, the kid turns eighteen in three months, and then it's none of your goddamned business if he goes to school.

So find him if you can, and if you do, you can goddamned well keep him!"

Anna's hand shook as she set down the phone. She didn't pick it up again, but went into the bathroom. She opened the medicine cabinet. There. Her mother's pills. She took out the prescription vial and set it on the edge of the sink. Then she went back to her room.

She wanted the diary tape. She thought there would be just enough space left at the end for a message. Even now in one part of her mind, absurdly, she kept worrying what she would say. If she could think of something good enough. She stuck her finger in the hub of one reel and tried to turn it, to wind up the loose tape. It wound a little way, then kinked and resisted.

Who was this message supposed to be for, her mother? Then her mother would hear all the other pathetic whining and pseudo-poetic ramblings on the tape, which she had vowed never to erase. She would hear about Dex.

Besides, what could she say to a person whose life she was preparing to destroy with grief and guilt? Of course her mother would blame herself, she'd see everything that happened to Anna as the result of some failure in her own love. Anna didn't think it was her mother's fault that she could no longer feel that love. Perhaps she'd outgrown it. Perhaps this was what it meant to be, finally, grownup—everything that had mattered to you before got lost, or became pointless.

Like poetry. Like her own unfinished poem about the shell, that was on the tape. Utterly pointless. The shell was empty, the creature inside departed. She might open door after door—or smash them down, what difference did it make? Every room she entered was alike, cold and deserted. Or filled with writhing forms and splashed with blood.

A sudden appalling memory of Dex ambushed her. Dex, with his hands on her throat. His own dark flesh purpling with excitement. Anna's guts twisted like scorching plastic. She had to run to the bathroom.

There, later, she pulled out the tape yard after yard, filling the sink with its slippery loops. When it was all unwound, every last bit, she took a bottle of nail-polish remover from the cabinet and poured it out over the tape.

Now it's all spoiled, she thought.

She stared down at the dispirited mess in the sink. She'd pictured something more drastic, like the tape would blacken and shrivel, emitting hellish fumes. It looked just like a handful of dead seaweed. She scooped it into the toilet bowl and flushed.

Just before leaving the apartment, she emptied the vial of pills into her pants pocket.

Anna trudged downhill, hands in her pockets, rolling the pills between her fingers. She crossed the highway. She wandered for hours, up and down residential streets, behind the Thriftway, around the edge of the ball park.

A softball game was in progress there. A bat cracked. Kids screamed in excitement. The park lights were beginning to shimmer in the summer dusk.

Anna came to the burned-out Horace S. Hurlbutt School. By now her steps dragged with exhaustion.

She stared up at the roofless silhouette of the building. The doors had been boarded over, of course, and the basement windows. But some of the upper windows, too high to be reached from the ground, stood open and glassless. She could see the sky through them, pale at the end of a hot day. It gave the building a two-dimensional look, like the painted backdrop of a ruin in a play.

She found one corner where a large crack yawned in the brick wall. A lot of bricks had fallen out, leaving a jagged cutout like a flight of giant steps that reached from the roof line almost to the ground. Somebody had leaned a wooden barricade here, which made it relatively easy for her to climb up and set her hands on a low place in the wall. By hauling herself up on her stomach, she could get inside.

She wasn't the first, either. Two guys sprawled on the floor of the gutted room and drank out of Orange Royale pop cans. Anna knew who they were. Shawn Kreizman had been in her freshman Global Studies class. His father ran an empire of video rental stores. The military-haircut type was a Brandon somebody. They called to her to join them. Brandon let her drink out of his can, which was half full of vodka.

The vodka brought the shadows of the old building to life. This room had been the library. Anna remembered the librarian, an astringent old lady with a ropy neck and a bosom so massive it rested on the counter before her like Webster's Unabridged. Anna, whose own breasts in sixth grade had begun to swell and grow tender, used to hate standing at the checkout counter, as if everybody looking at them together could see how they shared a painful weakness.

Brandon and Shawn told dirty jokes. Beyond the crack and wheeze of boys' laughter Anna could hear birds settling for the night in the ruined building. She drank more vodka.

Brandon kissed her. He had the soft beginnings of a mustache. His breath was warm and vomit-sweet. Shawn wandered off to pitch bits of brick against the wall. Brandon whispered that a girl who put her tongue out like Anna when she kissed must really want it.

Anna turned away and wiped her mouth with her fingers. They were dirty and bitter-tasting, like rust.

Brandon pulled her down beside him on the ground. He rolled so he lay partway on top of her, his leg over hers. He rubbed his body over hers. He was heavy. She could barely draw breath.

Anna thought, did it really matter if she had sex with Brandon? True, he was disgusting. He probably didn't like her much, either. They were just two random floaters in a cosmic void. It would all be over in a few minutes, anyway.

He said, "You have really great tits, you know that?" He forced his fingers inside her bra.

But he had to roll off a little to pull her up on her side, so he could get at the bra fastening in the back.

"Wait," Anna said. "I have some pills." She sat up and reached for the vodka pop can. Vodka and pills, how *banal*. She wished she knew how that word was supposed to be pronounced.

Brandon lay watching her, his face dopy and tender. "All my women got to have great tits," he said. "I don't look at any other kind."

Anna poured the drink out over his head. The orange stain crept through his buzz cut like a scalp disease.

She jumped to her feet and backed away. He was wiping his head, his face.

"Bitch!" he shouted.

In another second he'd get up and hit her. Anna ran to the corner where the wall came down like giant steps. She began to climb. Below her she heard Brandon yelling that she was a crazy bitch, that she was going to fall.

"What are you, some kind of virgin? I know you're not a virgin!"

Anna worked her way around the top of the wall, setting her feet carefully heel-to-toe. In places she could look down two stories through the ruined floor to wet black pits that had once been the boiler room, or the basement music room. The cool air of evening carried the smell of damp rot and charred wood and sour concrete.

She came to a gap where the top of a window had broken away. This was Miss Crandall's sixth-grade room. She could make out traces of the "Progress of Mankind" mural on the front wall. There used to be a companion piece, "Our First Thanksgiving," in Mrs. Mann's room across the hall.

Somewhere nearby a bird shifted its wings in a crack of ruined masonry, a sound like a throat cleared in the stillness before an orchestra begins to play.

Anna took a standing leap across the empty window frame and made it. One more step and a bit of mortar rubble rolling under her shoe brought her to her knees. She clung to the top of the wall, the rush of fear burning tracks to her fingertips. She couldn't see the ground on either side because it was getting dark and her eyes were filled with tears and the smoke of alcohol.

Someone was calling her name from the ruins of Miss Crandall's room. She could see his pale shirt and his face with the mouth open, like the place where a brick was missing. It was Dylan. Jeff.

She called, "I can't get down!"

"Yes, you can. Slip your legs around this side," he told her. "I can catch you."

"It's too dark!"

"I can see you fine, Anna."

She slid around and dropped. She passed through his waiting arms like the wind, like a shower of gold, like a ton of bricks. They lay side by side in Miss Crandall's room, giggling in wheezy bursts between gasping for breath.

Anna rolled over and clutched his shirt front. "I want you to say you love me. *Just say it*," she cried. "I don't care if it's not true!"

"I love you," he said. "I always tell you the truth."

She flopped onto her back and laughed till the tears rolled down her cheeks.

Dylan lay quietly beside her. Eventually he asked, "Finished now?"

"Yeah. Thanks . . ." She looked up at the pale evening sky above the ruined walls. "It's so deep. How did you get down here?"

"Through the door, duh." He told her the floor in the corridor was bad, but it was still possible to make it from the library, if you stuck close to the wall.

"Were you looking for me?" she asked.

"Of course." He'd gone home, hoping to borrow a couple of bills for gas. "And my mom was all over me about somebody called. It took me a while to figure out she meant you."

So he'd phoned her place and talked to her mother. Anna's mother told him he was the second guy who'd called looking for Anna that night, and where the hell was she anyway, because she was supposed to be home eating dinner with her mom and her mom's fiancé. Plus, she'd kept going on about what did Anna put in the toilet.

Dylan figured the other guy who'd called had to be Thorn, which meant she wasn't with him. So then he'd gone hunting.

"But what made you look here?"

"No particular reason. I tried a bunch of other places first." He'd just been prowling around after checking out the park and stopped to talk to a guy he saw chipping bricks out of the wall. The guy said maybe he'd seen Anna inside, earlier.

Dylan said he'd better take her home now, unless there was someplace she'd rather go. "You want a hand up?"

"Thanks. I must look disgusting." She wiped at her face with the backs of her hands.

"Only a little streaky," he said. "I left Nicole over by the ball park. I didn't want her too close, in case the cops would cruise by and get suspicious."

Anna stopped wiping. "What are you talking about, Nicole?"

"I told you. I parked her over by—"

"What are you talking about!"

"My car." He stared at her blankly. "You idiot, you don't mean you never figured out that's just what I call the car?"

"Your mother said you were sleeping at Nicole's."

"*In* Nicole, maybe. I do that some nights when stuff gets too weird at my house. Well, pretty much every night since that scene at County."

Anna felt suddenly too weak to stand. She had to lean against him. She whined against his chest, "Why did you lie to me? Why did you always lie?"

"I didn't lie! About my name? You just heard it wrong, is all." He swallowed. She could hear the sound go down his throat.

"O.K., so I wanted a chance to talk with you. I saw you down at the river that time, and it was just like, *gong*. Like, *oh, man* . . . And you came right up to me and took my hand . . . I didn't care what I said!"

He brought up his arms as if to hold her as she stood against him, but they got stuck halfway. His hands made little sawing motions in the air.

Anna stepped back. "You told me a bunch of lies about Nicole!"

"Well, what was I supposed to say? You'd just told me about Thorn. I saw how you were about that poor fuck down by the river! You despised him for being such a needy jerk. *That's why*—" His body seemed to spasm. He gasped, reached out, and pulled her back against him. He rubbed his face blindly in her hair. "I lied so you wouldn't think I was the same. Just one more desperate fool."

So this was it, Anna thought. This was how they came together. She looked up at him in amazement. Her hair still stuck to his cheek. Her lips parted to make some comment—not that it mattered, what she said now. They both knew.

"Hey, look—the tease found herself another sucker!"

Anna screamed. She couldn't help it. She swung around and saw Brandon and Shawn crowding through the classroom door.

"Heard you guys talking," said Shawn. Under the shadow of the doorway, his teeth gleamed in a wet smile.

Dylan said, "I don't think we need you pig-asses here."

"There's room for everybody, I guess," said Shawn. "We'll just get in line till you finish."

Brandon and Shawn bumped into each other, staggering and honking with laughter. Brandon started toward Anna, but Dy-

Ian stepped between them and shoved him away. Brandon spun halfway around, then swung back with his fist raised.

Dylan pushed him down on the floor.

"Jerk," he said.

Shawn cackled insanely. "Gonna fight?" He bounced around with his fists up, punching the air. "Hey, hey! Gonna fight!"

Anna said, "Please let's go, Dylan, *please.*"

She started to pull him away. She could barely move her legs, she was so burdened with foreknowledge. There would be a fight. Somehow Dylan would wind up arrested. Terrible words would spew from their mouths. She would lose him again.

Brandon got on all fours, then shoved his butt up and brought himself, swaying, to his feet. He was mumbling, "*Shit,* man . . . shit! About broke my butt bone, man . . ." Anna could see his Adam's apple working.

Shawn kept bouncing around, chanting, "Hey—gonna fight? Fight!" He picked up a loose brick from the floor and brandished it in the air.

"I don't want to fight," said Dylan.

"I'm going to kill him," Brandon said.

They all stood still. Frowning, Anna looked around at their faces, set in expressions of rage, or surprise, or scorn. It was the way Brandon stood more than his words that made her understand—hand raised, feet apart, shoulders twisted sideways—a shooter's stance, copied from TV, probably. He was pointing a gun at Dylan. The gun must have been a small one, because she could barely see it, engulfed in Brandon's wavering fist.

Shawn had frozen on tiptoe, in mid-bounce. He rocked back on his heels. "Are you fucking crazy?"

"What's the matter," Brandon taunted him, "you never killed a man before?"

"No, and neither did you. So shut the fuck up!"

"Yeah, well, there's always a first time."

An unexpected bubble of laughter burst from Anna's lips. Immediately the gun swung around to point at her.

"You think that's funny, bitch?"

Anna shook her head, but she had to cover her mouth to keep more bubbles from escaping. Half an hour ago, she'd been thinking of killing herself. Now here was somebody else all ready to do it for her, and she didn't even feel grateful. When she brought her hand away from her face, it was wet with tears.

Dylan said to Anna, as if he was just making regular conversation, "Lie on the floor, and keep your head down. Don't look."

He started walking slowly away from her, toward Brandon. The gun point slewed around to him again.

"If you think for one minute you can kill me with that cap pistol," Dylan said, "before I get to you, and rip your throat out with my teeth—and swallow it—you better think again. If you know how."

Brandon backed away. Dylan lunged at him. Shawn threw his brick. It caught Dylan on the point of his elbow. Dylan folded, grunting, over the hurt. Brandon fired, but the shot went high, stinging into the brick wall.

Brandon swung the gun around at the walls, the sky. He fired wildly. Anna screamed and dropped down on the floor. It was all over in a few seconds. The sound of gunshots still echoed round inside the walls, or inside Anna's skull. Her hands stung where bits of shattered brick had struck as she held them over her head. Her legs jerked with the sudden release of tension. She coughed out dust.

Anna looked for Dylan, but it was Brandon she saw, down on his knees, clutching his stomach. He was only spewing up vodka and terror.

Dylan sat behind him, against the wall. He had his knees up, kind of resting his head on his bent knees. Anna called to him.

With a strangled sob, or retch, Brandon heaved himself up and stumbled out the door. Anna could hear him sobbing and cursing down the corridor. Shawn, too, had disappeared.

Anna crawled over to sit beside Dylan. On the floor by the wall she found the gun, where Dylan must have dropped it after taking it from Brandon. Thinking back, Anna realized she'd only counted four shots. There might be more left in the gun. Then she also had to put her head between her knees as boiling nausea and even fiercer pride churned her stomach.

She rubbed her sweaty face on Dylan's sleeve. "Hey," she said. "It's over. You can look now."

His hands covered his face. He didn't answer.

"Dylan? Jeff . . . ? Are you O.K.?" She stood and touched his shoulder.

When he still didn't speak, she took hold of one hand and peeled it back from his face.

"I said, are you O—" *Ohh.*

His hand was full of blood. A cup of blood. It seeped through his fingers now, over his wrist. He covered his face again with his hand, but Anna had seen the gaping cut, the bloodied slime where his eye had been.

THE CHARIOT

This was Anna's nightmare, the shots, her mind a panic blank, her legs unwilling to function. The only difference was that she was not the person dying.

Dylan had dropped his other hand across his knees. She took it and held it in the warm crook of her neck, between her cheek and shoulder. It lay there leaden and cold.

"Listen to me," she commanded. "You can't die yet. You have to wait till I get help."

Dylan opened his one eye. "I'm not going to die," he said. "But don't go."

"I have to get help!"

"O.K. . . . Then I'll go with you."

He braced his feet and pushed himself up, scraping his back along the wall for support. Anna pulled his arm around her shoulders.

She saw at once they wouldn't be able to walk like that in the corridor. It was almost pitch-dark in there, though it was open to the sky. She could make out gleaming patches on the floor, and inky pools—puddles? Or holes?

Anna told Dylan she'd go in front.

"*Yes,*" she said, when he tried to protest. "Because I can see better. Put your left hand on my shoulder. I don't care if it's bloody, idiot! Keep your other shoulder against the wall."

She worked out a kind of rocking gait, sliding one foot ahead, then leaning forward on it to test the floor, before following up with her other foot. Dylan stepped behind her, rocking to keep in balance with her. In one place she could feel the whole floor slanting sharply down toward the center of the corridor. They kept their backs against the wall and shuffled sideways, holding hands. Anna dug the pills out of her pocket and threw them into the dark, hoping there was a hole there.

They found the library deserted. Peering over the broken wall, Anna saw the bright stripes of the wooden barrier lying flat on the ground. Brandon or Shawn must have kicked it over on the way out. Anna dropped over first, with the intention of putting the barrier back for Dylan.

But he followed too close behind. He didn't realize she hadn't set the foothold in place. He fell awkwardly, knocking Anna down with him. She lay on the dirt holding him until his jagged panting quieted, until she felt his blood soaking into her shirt. It was so warm she hardly noticed at first.

They started back across the cracked asphalt toward the ball park. She didn't think too much about where they were going, or what she had to do, but just put one foot after the other, grateful to feel his weight across her shoulders, his breath still warm in her hair.

The parking strip by the ball field was empty except for Nicole. Dylan had left her way down at the end, next to the sign that read *This Park Closes at 10 PM*. It was later than that, then.

Dylan leaned with both hands against the car door. "You drive," he said.

"I can't drive! I don't have any license."

"I'll tell you what to do."

"Dylan, we can go in any one of these houses around here and just tell them to call 911."

"At night?" He stretched a grin across his mutilated face. Every part of him that she could see, face, hair, hands, shirt, was blotched and caked with blood and dirt and smeary soot.

He said, "You look the same . . . scary, at the door. They'll shoot . . ."

He appeared to be sliding down the side of the car. Anna wrapped her arms around him.

"Dylan, stay on your feet till I get the door open. I can't lift you."

Once in the car, Dylan slumped against the door, not speaking. Anna reached into his pocket for the keys.

"But I'm not driving to the hospital," she said. "That would mean the freeway, and there's no point in killing us both now. There's a police station just up the road."

She feared he'd lost consciousness, but he roused when she jumped the seat forward, cramming his knees under the dashboard. He tried to tell her how to start the car.

"I took Driver's Ed," she interrupted him. "Fasten your seat belt."

Nicole, darling Nicole, was not a jealous girlfriend. She started sweetly. Thank God for an automatic transmission.

Anna put her in reverse. The car shot halfway across the street, groaned, then lurched forward, climbing partway up the curb to kiss a mailbox before Anna got her straightened. Anna figured she'd stick to the middle of the street from now on.

"Lights," Dylan murmured. "Put on your lights. Take the next right."

Nicole wandered a little while Anna searched for the lights. But she achieved the turn. Anna noticed in time to stop at the sign a block up. Then disaster: a main road, with traffic.

"Left turn," Dylan said.

Anna pulled slowly left. She could barely see over the dashboard in this car. An oncoming minivan blared its horn.

"Fuck 'em," Dylan said. "They'll get out of the way. Got to figure, their paint . . . worth more than mine."

"Shut up," Anna told him. "Don't distract me."

But then his silence distracted her more. She glanced over at him. His hand lay loosely on the seat, no longer covering his wound. The wound itself was a featureless dark. A bullet might still be inside there, lodged halfway to his brain.

She jabbed her toe at the gas pedal. The car surged to thirty miles an hour. Sweat glued her fingers to the steering wheel. She saw other cars way ahead in her lane. Dylan said nothing. Thirty-five miles an hour.

"Dylan? Are you still O.K.? Jeff? I don't even know what to call you!"

"Call me Dillon, like you always did . . . only now . . . say it with your *a*'s open."

"Is that supposed to be a pun? You're delirious!"

"I'm happy."

"Oh my god," said Anna. "Look—is that a police car? Two

ahead of us." She powered down the window and shouted out, "Stop! Emergency!"

Nicole swerved. Anna pounded on the horn. "Oh, why don't they pay attention?"

"Anna, slow down. You're climbing the ass of the guy ahead. He's tapping his brakes to warn you—"

Anna leaned with her full weight on the horn. Unconsciously she also pressed harder on the accelerator.

The car ahead veered to the side of the road, bucking as it bounced off the curb. Nicole flew by at fifty miles an hour.

"Anna, brake! *Brake!*"

The back of the police car loomed. Anna fumbled with her foot for the other pedal. Dillon grabbed the emergency brake and pulled. Nicole sashayed her rear end.

Anna had an instant's vision of a cop's white face through the rear window of his car before they crashed.

The next week, Anna's mother took time off work to ferry Anna on an endless round of sessions with the police, youth counselors, a lawyer, a judge. In the end, no criminal charges were brought against Anna or Dillon. A judge in traffic court ordered Anna to attend safe-driving classes two nights a week for the whole month of August. He also recommended family counseling. Dillon got cited for not having car insurance. Nicole was impounded.

Brandon bargained for a guilty plea to assault and weapons charges in juvenile court. That way, since he was only sixteen, he avoided prosecution as an adult. Anna honestly couldn't understand how anyone could think he'd acted like an adult, anyway. She didn't know what, if anything, would happen to Shawn. His father's lawyers were still working on it.

Dillon spent two nights in the hospital while doctors stitched up his eye and the gash in the lid. No bullet had struck him. A fragment of shattered brick had slashed through the lid to the golden-brown iris beneath. They could not save the sight in his eye.

Ten days later Dillon had to go back in the hospital for plastic surgery, and to repair a ripped tendon so the eyelid would close normally. After that, there was nothing more the doctors could do, at least not on the state health plan. Expensive reconstructive surgery would be required, they said, if he ever wanted to wear a prosthesis. The hospital suggested setting up a fund for private donations, but they didn't hold out too much hope.

Dillon said, *So what.* He liked the idea of a black patch, he figured it for a cheap leap to the front lines of cooldom. Someday, he said, he might get something really fancy to cover the scar—something sparkly, like maybe silver. Anna thought with luck he'd never be able to afford that.

Thorn phoned Anna at home the morning after Dillon got shot. The story was in the paper, with Anna's name. Walt Durban was staying at the apartment to handle phone calls and reporters. He wouldn't let Thorn speak to Anna.

Thorn called every day for the next week. At first Anna was too busy to see him. Then one afternoon after her mother had gone back to work he showed up unexpectedly at her front door.

He took her for a long drive through Woodland Park, then back to his apartment. They made love, the way they used to when everything was still new for her. Thorn was very patient, very gentle. But so much had changed in Anna's life recently she couldn't help that her thoughts were distracted. She couldn't respond properly.

Neither of them mentioned Pauline, who had gone to San Diego on vacation. Her father lived down there.

TWO OF CUPS

When Dillon went back for his second surgery, the one to repair his eyelid, Thorn drove Anna up to the hospital for a visit. Thorn even went in with her to Dillon's room. He stood quietly looking out the window while Anna and Dillon talked.

Dillon's surgery was scheduled for the next morning. Anna thought he seemed edgy. She felt thankful when a nurse came in and told them to keep the visit short. Dillon needed his rest, the nurse said.

Thorn said to Anna as they were leaving, "I noticed from the window there's a little garden with some roses . . . Why don't we go down and look for it?"

In the garden, cement paths led between clipped green lawns and patterned beds of roses. They sat together on a bench under an arbor of red roses. Anna thought, *This is where the doctors bring you, to pat your hand and tell you somebody's died.*

Thorn pulled down a bloom to try against Anna's dark hair. But it was overblown and shattered, raining crimson petals over her. He wiped one off her cheek.

He told her he had to go to New York. "I'll leave next week, and spend about ten days there. After that, where I go depends . . ."

"Depends," Anna repeated. "On what?"

"Mainly on you, Anna. I love you. You must know that."

Anna nodded and looked down at a rose petal she was teasing between her fingers. The color grew darker and the scent more vegetable as she crushed and smoothed it out again. She'd waited a lifetime to hear those words.

He said, "There must be some way I can take you with me, back to my other life. This last week, while you've been so distant from me, I've thought of little else. We could get you into some writer's program. New York has alternative schools, even colleges that might let you in as a special student."

He put his arm around her, stroked her cheek until he'd turned her face to his.

"New York is such a marvelous city," he said, "full of treasure, and terror, and delight. I want to show you all these things."

Her gaze faltered.

"Why do you look away? Are you still angry with me?"

"I'm just tired, really."

"You're so young. You're still looking for the fairy-tale ending."

"No, I'm not. I just . . . I just wanted a different kind of beginning, maybe."

"Then let's begin again. A new city, a new love . . . Tell me you want this," he said. He kissed the corner of her mouth, where a tiny smile flickered. "You have a sister in New York. Don't you ever come visit her?"

Anna's mouth twitched. It wasn't flirtatiousness, she was only trying not to cry. She'd always tried so hard not to break down in front of Thorn.

She said, "Vonda and I don't get along too well. And besides, my mother's getting married. I have to stay here for the wedding."

Pain etched delicate lines in the corners of his mouth and between his brows. Anna thought perhaps if he went through his life laughing and joyous, like Dillon, he'd only grow pudgy and dull. She was surprised by the cruelty of her thought.

"You're thinking something," he said. "Tell me."

"I was thinking . . . something we have in common, maybe. Sadness makes you beautiful."

He let her go, suddenly, as if her touch scorched him. Anna studied the lines of his face, making a pattern of them, abstract yet living. Like the form of a poem.

"I'm losing you, aren't I?" he said. "I can see it in your eyes, the way you look at me, so full of wonder. You looked like that on the first night I saw you—as if you'd only just stepped down from another world. Now you've gone back there. I never touched you, never changed you at all."

Anna shook her head no. How could he believe that?

But he went on, "The next man who comes to love you will find the same shining gaze . . . the same virgin . . . the same pale muse."

He invented me for himself, Anna thought, *just like I invented him.*

They sat for a while longer under the arbor, until a breeze brought a scattering of raindrops to shake the rose leaves and remind Thorn that he'd left the top down on the car. He said they'd better go.

"You go," Anna said. "I'll catch the bus home."

"Anna!" Disbelief widened his eyes. "Will I see you again before I leave? When?"

"I . . . I don't really think so. No." She stood up, brushing away the last petals clinging to her skirt. "Goodbye, Thorn."

She took a few steps along the cement path. Her legs felt new, as if the bones had not yet hardened for use.

He called after her, *"Where are you going?"*

She couldn't tell if it was grief or rage that twisted up his voice. She'd never know, unless she turned around to look. She didn't turn. She repeated over and over to herself as she kept walking, *I won't tell you. I won't tell you.*

When she reached the corner of the hospital building, she began to run.

She took the elevator up to Dillon's floor. There was nobody else in the car but she wedged herself into a corner. She jammed the backs of her fists against the walls and pushed— pushed till her muscles locked. The cords stood out on her neck. Her voice, uttering pointless noises, squeezed down to a whine.

The elevator doors opened. Anna stepped out. Her arms floated up all by themselves, magically, like wings.

Mrs. Dillon stood waiting to take the elevator down. She wore mauve lipstick, generously applied, and clutched her purse with both hands to her bosom.

She said, "Oh my lord, it's Jeffie's girlfriend. How are you, honey? You look just like a little butterfly." She smiled, revealing mauve-streaked teeth. "Jeffie said you left."

"I had to come back for a minute . . ."

"Well, that's good. You cheer him up for me, honey, O.K.?"

The elevator doors began to close. Anna stepped back to

hold them for Mrs. Dillon, but the lady made no move to get in.

She said, "Yeah, Jeff's talked about you. You know, I always just wished he'd get a job, maybe a nice girlfriend . . . They'd take him anyplace, he's that smart. Dealerships, even, I told him."

"He needs to finish school," Anna said. The doors nudged at her back insistently.

"Now you sound like Family Services. I told him O.K., he can come home one more year, graduate the damn high school—but after that, I said, you get a full-time job, buster, or you're out of here! I ain't paying for him to camp on his butt at some goddamned college."

Anna said, "Mrs. Dillon, do you want this elevator?"

"Thanks, honey." She squeezed past Anna into the car. "Jeff ever tell you about his dad? He was some wild kind of god-damned poet. Half the time you couldn't understand a damned word he said, and he was foreign, too. I told Jeffie, stick to what you can do with your hands and keep your damned trap shut. I said—"

The doors cut off the rest of her tirade. Anna watched the elevator light marking down the floors. Then she went to find Dillon's room.

A nurse was just coming out. She told Anna visiting hours were over.

"I left my bag here," Anna said. "It has my bus pass . . ."

Dillon called from the room, "Is that Anna? Hey, you left your stuff here!"

The nurse eyed Anna grudgingly, then stepped aside to let her go in.

Dillon's face, the part not covered by a molded plastic dressing, lit up as he saw her. He sat cross-legged, wearing a T-shirt and gym shorts that belonged on somebody fatter. His supper tray was on a swivel table over his bed. He pushed it aside. The nurse protested.

"I have to talk to my friend," Dillon said, "or I'll get post-operative stress and bleed."

"Your operation isn't until tomorrow."

"Pre-operative, then. I can already feel it starting to gush."

The nurse said he was too much. But she had her supper rounds to finish. She'd check back on him after that. "And I don't want to find you here when I do, young lady."

As soon as she'd gone, Dillon asked about Thorn. He didn't smile anymore.

Anna sat down on the bed beside Dillon's. It was empty and stripped. Dillon's roommate had been discharged that afternoon.

She said, "He's going back to New York."

"And what about you?"

"What about me? I'm all right here."

Dillon swung his legs off the bed and went to close the door. He wedged a visitor's chair under the handle. Then he came back and sat across from Anna. Their knees were close together. He could have stretched out his leg to touch hers, but he didn't. He kept his face turned so all she could see was the strange, cold, featureless plastic mask. In some ways, Anna thought, she knew no more than that about Dillon.

She said, "I really only did come to get my bag."

He looked over at the chair where it lay. There was his familiar face again. His eye was a bright tawny color. Anna thought how she'd wanted to touch those crinkling lines with her fingers. Maybe with her tongue.

He was saying, "What do you keep in there, anyway? I've always wondered about the junk girls put in their purses."

"Not a lot," she told him. "My bus pass, stuff like that. A hairbrush. Oh, and I brought the tarot cards."

"Great! You can tell my fortune."

"All right."

She got out the cards and shuffled while he smoothed out a place on his bedcovers.

"I saw your mother out in the hall," she said.

Dillon winced. "I hope it didn't get too intense."

"She talked about your father. You're supposed to cut the cards three times, then pass them to me."

He cut the cards, then made a big deal of scratching his nose around the edge of the dressing. His hand shielded the good part of his face.

He said, "In my family, drinking and poetry don't mix. My dad tried it, and see where it got him. So my mom sticks with the booze. Maybe I'll wind up ODing on poetry, you never know." He laughed self-consciously, still hiding his face.

"Now I don't know what to think," Anna said. "Thorn always told me the truth, and you hid stuff, right from the beginning."

"Maybe we ought to begin again."

"No, we can't do that."

"Let's begin in the middle, then. Or at the end, and work backwards. One day when I'm about ninety-six, I'll suddenly look at you and think, *Man! That girl is hot.* My last thought on earth."

"You are so full of it."

Anna started to lay out the cards. She named each one's position as she set it down.

"The page of wands stands for you. Maybe I should've chosen the knight, but I like the page better. This is the cover card. Next one's the basis of the situation. This is an influence that's passing away. This one's a possible outcome—"

"I like that one," Dillon interrupted. "Tell me about that one." It was the two of cups.

"Yeah, it's a good card," she said, then hesitated.

The two in the picture were a young man and a girl, fully dressed and crowned with wreaths. They toasted each other out of brimming goblets. The card meant kindred spirits, the beginning of a friendship or a love affair. Anna felt shy to talk about it.

He misinterpreted her silence.

"I guess it's no big thing, huh? Just a low number. I know, the important cards are supposed to be the ones with names, the what-do-you-call-them—?"

"The major arcana."

"Yeah. I didn't get any of those."

"You got the chariot, the basis of the situation. But, anyway, the major arcana aren't necessarily more important than the others," she told him. "Sometimes, if you get a bunch together in your reading, it just means you aren't taking control of your own life. Like you're letting outside forces run the whole show for you. But let me finish the layout. Then we'll go back and interpret."

The next card she drew was the fool, reversed.

"*Shit.* I always get that one! It's starting to haunt me. It's always the wrong way around."

"I can fix that," Dillon said. He reached out and turned the fool right side up.

"You can't do that!"

"Why not? I'm a wild card, I can do anything I want." He pointed to his bandaged face. "One-eyed jacks are wild."

"In poker, maybe."

"O.K., so let's play poker."

"With the tarot cards?"

Dillon flopped sideways across his bed and stretched his long arms and legs. "I hate all this lying around," he complained. "I want something to do."

His shorts rode low on his hips, so Anna could see the muscles of his stomach rising in clean hard bands between the pointy bones.

She looked away, at her unfinished layout. The two of cups seemed like a good place to start, even without the final outcome. She picked up the card and held it to her face, covering first one eye, then the other. One eye saw a shiny pink plastic blank. The other saw Dillon.

She thought, he must have grieved for the loss of his eye. He hadn't shown her his grief. Maybe he was trying to protect her from feeling guilty, because most of what happened had been her fault. Maybe he thought she didn't care.

She'd been so stupid, wrapped up in her own drama, she'd just assumed Dillon would always be there, like air to breathe . . . Until, for a while, he wasn't. She touched the corner of his good eye with her fingertip. How delicate a person was, right there. How easy to hurt.

She asked, "Is it O.K. if I kiss you?"

He put his hand over hers and moved it down so her fingers

brushed his mouth, then over, sliding around the cool plastic.

"You don't mind, with this?"

"Not if it doesn't hurt you."

She lay crosswise on the bed beside him, her head propped on her hand. She touched him lightly, learning him. Eyelid, lips, throat moving delicately under her fingers, hard ridges of the breast . . .

"I can feel your heart beating," she said.

His kiss was like she'd remembered, opening sweetly beneath hers. His next kiss grew hungry and delighting. He pulled her down to him, so his heartbeat tangled with her own.

She whispered, "Don't."

"I thought you wanted to."

"I don't know what I want!" Her throat clogged with fear, and desire. For so long she'd been in love with a man who didn't exist. Dillon seemed terrifyingly real.

She said, "I need time . . . maybe a lot of time."

He found her hand and held it over his heart again.

"Time is O.K.," he said.

"It is, isn't it?" she said. "Because, really, I hardly know you . . . or myself. I'm still thinking about all this."

"So am I," said Dillon. "I think it's a truly goddamned stupendous idea."